MEMO:
MARRY ME?

BY
JENNIE ADAMS

MILLS & BOON®

First published in Great Britain 2007
Harlequin Mills & Boon Limited,
Eton House, 18-24 Paradise Road, Richmond, Surrey TW9 1SR

© Jennifer Ann Ryan 2007

ISBN-13: 978 0 263 85432 9
ISBN-10:   0 263 85432 9

Set in Times Roman 12½ on 14¾ pt
02-0507-48554

Printed and bound in Spain
by Litografia Rosés, S.A., Barcelona

Jennie Adams believes a little of the author's life appears in every book. In the case of Lily Kellaway in this story it's list-making, and a deep admiration for those who face adversity on a daily basis and somehow remain so strong. This book is Jennie's tribute to you all.

Jennie loves to hear from her readers, and can be contacted via her website at www.jennieadams.net

Previous titles by this author:

THE BOSS'S CONVENIENT BRIDE
PARENTS OF CONVENIENCE
HER MILLIONAIRE BOSS

For Cheryl, whose courage, humour and strength inspire me constantly, and inspired the idea for Lily's story. Thanks for the working lunches, the laughs, and the internet jokes. You're a champion.

For Mary Hawkins. The mountains are inevitable. Thanks for climbing a little of this one with me.

And for my editor, Joanne Carr. Thanks so much.

CHAPTER ONE

'ARE you Zachary Swift?' Lily stood in the doorway of the spacious eighteenth-floor Sydney office, and pushed words up through a throat filled with fear. She hoped she sounded calm and rational, and not worried sick. 'I'm Lily Kellaway, owner and manager of Best Secretarial Agency. I'm here in response to your…concerns about my employee.'

He could refuse to speak to her. Could have her and her agency blackballed, and end her career just like that. Lily knew it, feared it, but if she wanted any chance to make this situation right she had to sound confident, a woman who could and *would* make things better.

'I'm Zach Swift, yes, and it's no idle accusation against Rochelle Farrer.' He sat at his desk, broad shoulders pressed into a black leather chair, confidence and assurance written in every line of his body.

Sydney's leaden April sky loomed behind him, viewed through a bank of plate-glass windows. Through a long, slim grill above those windows, the sounds of a city that never stopped emphasised his decisive words—vehicles possessing the roads below, the blast and clang of construction, a siren's blare.

Firm, determined sounds, when Lily only wanted to hear his deep voice softening, inviting her in to discuss this problem face to face.

'I don't dispute your accusation.' She wished she could disprove it, but, sadly, it was all true. 'But it's one that can be addressed. Amends can be made. The situation can be fixed.'

'Is that why you're here? To try to fix what happened? There's no turning back the clock.' Dark brows drew down. His lean, tanned face revealed his irritation. 'I think I made my feelings quite clear when we spoke by phone half an hour ago.'

She recalled the shock of that phone call very well. Dismay and embarrassment had robbed her of the ability to reason with him.

While she'd still been floundering, he had told her he wanted nothing more to do with her agency, and had hung up.

'You raised certain issues when you phoned.' The empty secretary's desk in the reception room at her back mocked her. Her fingers clenched around the notebook held in her left hand, and she prayed that he would listen. 'I'd like the chance to address those issues, now that I've had time to assimilate what's happened.'

Please, God, she wouldn't forget the speech rehearsed three times on the frantic taxi trip here.

'What's to address? I sacked your employee. I've sacked your agency. End of story.' With an irritated growl, he rose and stalked across the thick beige carpet until he stood before her.

Over six feet of annoyed, affronted male, and her agency was responsible for his anger. She quaked. But something else happened, too. Something quick and unexpected when her gaze zeroed in on thick-fringed hazel eyes. A mixture of curiosity and interest flowed through her, locked her breath in her throat. Shock and dismay followed. She couldn't be attracted to him? It must be some sort of nervous reaction, surely?

Yes, that must be it, and just as well, because all other facts aside she was too busy for a relationship with a man right now. Busy. Inadequate. Just look at your relationship with your parents, a silent voice interjected. 'All I ask is a few minutes of your time. If you'll hear me out, those minutes will be well invested.'

'Will they, Ms Kellaway? You seem very sure of that.'

Lily adjusted the weight of the tote bag slung over her shoulder, tugged her green skirt into place and smoothed the matching blazer. 'I have a solution.'

'Do you? For the past week I've been sexually stalked while your employee ignored her duties.' His narrowed eyes revealed his distaste. 'My working life has been thoroughly wrecked, culminating in this morning's episode. *Your* agency is responsible for that, and you want to *solve* my problem?'

Lily drew a sharp breath. Something mellow and male drifted across her senses. Cedar wood and citrus, heated by warm man. 'I do apologise…' The words trailed off as her attention seemed to shift of its own volition to the black leather sofa in the corner.

He followed her gaze, and his lips thinned. 'Were you aware I would walk in on that particular sight today? Perhaps your agency condones such behaviour in its temp secretaries?'

'I was certainly *not* aware that Rochelle had behaved in such a way, or that she might do so.' Lily had no doubt that this indelible piece of conversation would stick like a barnacle to the inside of her head. 'If I'd known, I never would have employed her. Until now, I've not had a whiff of trouble from any of my employees.'

'Then how did it happen, Ms Kellaway?' He strode away, clasped the edges of the desk in long-fingered hands. An intense and focussed scrutiny demanded her answer. 'How was it that I walked into my office this morning to find Rochelle Farrer waiting naked for me on my sofa?'

Lily's hand shook as she snared a few errant strands of hair and pushed them back off her face. Rochelle had believed if she'd stripped off and waited this man would leap at the chance to have her, and afterwards to keep her.

She hadn't hesitated to say so, when Lily had confronted her by phone as she'd rushed here to try to put things to rights. 'Rochelle… appeared to be under the misapprehension that she could, uh—'

'Marry a rich husband and live off his wealth for the rest of her life?' He inserted the words with freezing helpfulness. 'And she only needed to throw herself at her potential victim to get her wish?'

'Well, yes.' Lily's mouth tightened into a stiff pucker. He might be angry, but the interview with Rochelle hadn't exactly been pleasant for her, either! 'I didn't know Rochelle would sell herself that way for the chance to become a wealthy man's wife. When I interviewed her, she seemed very genuine and businesslike.'

His prolonged silence made her want to fidget. And she wanted desperately to use her notebook to try to get down what they had said so far.

At least she only had to be here long enough to get him to agree to take Deborah on. Then she could return to the safety of running her agency from her small apartment. To days filled with the transcription typing that allowed her to remain out of harm's way, where her shortcomings couldn't get her into trouble. To only venturing out when she felt up to the challenge.

He examined her with disconcerting thoroughness. Eventually, he dipped his head slightly in acknowledgement. 'Surprisingly, I believe you.'

'Thank you.' Her knees sagged with the weight of that gratefully received reprieve. 'I'm so pleased to hear you say—'

'Not that it changes anything.' He burst her bubble of hope expertly and without waste of words. 'Rochelle didn't exactly deliver on your agency's promise of "a reliable secretary with previous experience in busy, challenging office environments", did she?'

'No. She didn't.'

And, while Lily stood in his doorway and attempted to sort this out, she was at a distinct disadvantage. 'I respect your concerns, and the distaste you must feel for all that you've been through. But I have an offer to make that can turn this situation into something more positive. I believe it will be in your company's best interests to hear it.'

After a long moment, he sighed and waved an arm towards the studded visitor's chair that faced his desk. 'All right, I suppose I can spare you a few minutes in comfort. If we're lucky, the phone might even stay quiet for that long.'

He didn't clarify, 'a few minutes to settle this permanently before I contact a more reliable agency and get them to send me a decent secretary', but she had no doubt he thought it.

'Thank you.' She started towards the chair. 'All I want is enough of your time to allow me to resolve this matter.'

'As far as I'm concerned the matter is…' His words faltered. His gaze locked on the movement of her hips beneath the conservative green skirt. His eyelids dropped, but not before she saw the mixture of knowledge and curiosity that confirmed his interest in her—willing or not.

If she'd felt a certain tingling *something* just now too, well, that was because being here gave her the fidgets. It was nerves that sent ripply feelings down her spine, and made her skin feel too tight, certainly not some reaction to him.

Even as she denied any interest in him, a small part of her catalogued the harsh face with its angry frown line and strong jaw, and the thick, dark brown hair.

Lily shook her head and dragged her

thoughts back to business. She would finish this. Then she would leave, with a dignified, impersonal handshake. This…interest, or whatever it was, would quickly be forgotten.

'I hope you don't expect to be paid for the week Rochelle stalked me around the office, ignored her work and made a mess of everything?' Zachary gifted her with a glare from beneath his brows.

'Certainly not.' That loss of revenue was only one of her worries right now. 'I would never ask such a thing of a valued employer.'

'But you're here to ask something.'

'Yes, and please believe me when I say I do realise how serious this is.' This was the most important part of her speech. The part that had to convince him to give Best Secretarial Agency a second chance.

Yet now she struggled to drag the words from the recesses of her mind, and panic rippled. She needed this man's forgiveness. If not that, then at least another chance to show him that her agency could live up to expectations.

'You have every right to be affronted and offended. Repulsed, even.' Her pencil flew across the notebook, recorded the basics of the conversation in the special, easy code learned through endless repetition.

If the matter is in any way important, always keep a record. Even before her mentor had told her that, she had done so. Religiously, in fact, since she'd discharged herself from the hospital. Since she'd walked away from her parents' shame, and from her broken dreams.

Zach inclined his head. 'It was a shock to enter my office and find…that. If I'd had anyone with me—'

'It would have been even worse. I agree. And I didn't mean you'd be *repulsed*, repulsed. That is, I'm sure the media testimonies to your, um, interest in women are true.'

Oh, good heavens. Did she have to go on about that? She really needed to focus!

'I'm relieved to know that the Powers That Be acknowledge my healthy heterosexuality.' Sarcasm dripped from each word, but something in his glance revealed that at least some small degree of that healthy maleness was currently focussed on her.

She came back to earth with a thump when he finished saying something and waited expectantly.

Press rewind, and play back—no. Nothing. Whatever his words, she couldn't remember them. Just that one little slip in concentration…

A familiar icy feeling stole through her.

Drat it, Lily. Keep your mind where it should be! Give yourself at least half a chance to get a positive outcome from this.

'Yes, well, um…' Oh, why had Rochelle done this awful thing? And with absolutely no sense of shame or remorse, before or after the event. 'I apologise fully on behalf of Best Secretarial Agency for this unacceptable occurrence. I've let Rochelle go.'

'I doubt you'll consider it a loss.' His mild nod of approval was at least something.

'No. Most likely not.' She might as well be honest about that. Her pencil continued to fly. 'But let me present my offer.'

He leaned forward, his expression intent and far from acquiescent. 'I'd appreciate it if you'd keep it short.'

'You're in need of a replacement secretary. I'm ready and able to provide one.' Each fact went into her notebook. 'To ensure there will be no further difficulties, I want to send Deborah Martyn to you. Deb is my second-in-command, a middle-aged, reliable woman with a lot of office experience behind her.'

She drew a hurried breath and went on. 'I can have Deb here within…' She checked her book rapidly and found the note stating Deborah's availability. 'Within the hour. As an added incentive, I'd like to offer an extra two weeks of work, free of charge, after the end of the existing contract. It can't be easy to obtain a good secretary at a moment's notice. This will save you the time and effort of that search.'

Her breath stuck in her throat until she forced her lungs to move again. 'I presume you haven't already made alternative arrangements?'

'I haven't had time.' He gave a mirthless laugh. 'Let's say I agreed to consider a replacement, which I haven't.'

She had expected some opposition, and sat forward, pencil poised. 'Yes?'

'I don't think it would be wise to take on another unknown female, after the problems I've just experienced. Now if, instead of Deborah Martyn, you could give me a male secretary? Skilled? Fully experienced?'

He emphasised each question with a tap of his

finger against the blotter on his desk. 'Preferably one with a wife and kids at home. Someone you can guarantee will be here to work and nothing else. I might consider that. *Might.*'

No male employees, married or otherwise, existed in her retinue of available staff. She had no one to offer but Deborah—a wonderful worker, but definitely female. 'Not a male, no, but I can assure you Deborah is a very happily married—'

'Woman?' He ran a hand over the back of his neck, said it as though the very word were a plague. Yet his gaze lingered on her.

'A very responsible woman,' Lily began, only to be stopped by an upraised hand.

He shifted his focus beyond her to the outer office. 'From my standpoint, it would seem safer to approach a different agency. One more established, perhaps, so that the reputation it's built can truly be trusted.'

'Please. I want the good will of your company.' She had told herself she wouldn't beg, but knew she was close to it right now.

The 'girls' relied on her to keep them in work. All five were great women, and all needed the money brought in through their efforts. They were a tight little band, formed within the first month of the agency's opening nine months ago. Rochelle had come later, and had never really fitted in. Lily should have asked herself the reason for that, should have remembered to check all Rochelle's references thoroughly, and perhaps she might have thought twice about taking Rochelle on at all!

Now she owed it to her girls to fix this problem. And she admitted she needed to do this for herself, too. What would she have left if her agency went under? 'I'll do whatever I need to, in order to regain your good will.'

'No. I'm sorry.' He got to his feet. 'I appreciate the offer, but I can't accept it.'

He couldn't end the interview. Not yet.

'I'll raise the added free service to a month.' Lily stood, too. How her budget would stretch to such a commitment, she had no idea, but she had to convince him.

'You're certainly determined.' His gaze bored into hers with shrewd evaluation, and again with that hint of not entirely concealed male interest. 'And probably worried sick that I'll sue your company.'

Her heart fluttered in response to that look, but the flutter stopped abruptly as she absorbed his words. She feigned a calm she didn't feel. Shook her head. 'Not at all. I—'

She had considered it. Indeed, she had almost made herself ill thinking about it on the way here. If he took legal action, her agency could be deemed culpable of all sorts of awful things and might sink in a sea of murky corporate waters, never to be seen again.

If he denigrated her agency to his business colleagues, that alone would bring about the same result. Neither option was acceptable. 'Is that what you have in mind?'

'No.'

Just that. Flat. Unequivocal. Decided, she suspected, before he even brought the matter up.

He went on, a considering look in the backs of his eyes. 'But I'm impressed by your commitment to your agency, and by your resourcefulness. I've decided there *is* a way you can placate me.'

'Anything.' Words poured out. 'A line of dedication to you on my tombstone. Jemima's firstborn kitten—if I don't manage to get her spayed before that happens. All Betty's eggs for a year.'

She sounded too desperate, managed at

least to stop herself before she admitted to her eBay addiction, too. Heat stung her cheeks. 'Well, naturally you wouldn't care about any of that, but what did you have in mind? If it's within my power to do so, I'll make it happen.'

'Jemima? Betty?' He murmured the names, and for a brief moment warm humour lit his eyes.

There was something so appealing about a man who could smile…

Then he shook his head, and the expression vanished. 'Initially, all I thought I wanted— needed—was someone to keep things in basic good order while my regular secretary took her long-service leave.'

'Yes.' Her vigorous nod made her hair swing against her cheeks. 'I understood those were your requirements when you first contacted us.'

He took a step forward. Reached one hand towards her cheek, stopped, shoved both hands into his pockets. 'Things have changed.'

'I'm afraid I don't quite understand.' She tightened her grip on the red and black pencil. Had he really been about to stroke her face? Her skin begged her to make it happen.

'A woman in your position would have to

be well-versed in all aspects of office skills?' he prompted.

'Well, yes, I am.' Her pencil traversed the page at warp speed, making her odd-looking squiggles. Why make this personal—about her, specifically? Fresh unease built up.

'You'd have worked on a number of temporary jobs, Ms Kellaway?' A muscle in his jaw tightened, and his dark gaze shifted just once to her mouth before moving away. 'Do you still do that?'

It took all her effort not to raise a hand to her lips. To touch them, as though, by simply looking at them, he had changed their texture or shape and she needed to feel that change for herself. 'I keep my hand in, yes, with short assignments that don't take too much away from my other responsibilities.'

Assignments that allowed her to appear in a good light to those business people she chose for the purposes of keeping her skills fresh. 'My commitment to the agency doesn't allow for more than that.'

That was true, too, if not all of the truth.

'If circumstances demanded it, you could do more. You would adapt. I suspect you would be good at that.' His words held a husky timbre that made her wonder just what sort of adaptation he was thinking about.

Then he gave a brief nod. 'So here's *my* proposition. I want you in this office, to sort out my problems and deal with my backlog.'

With each statement, her eyes widened. A mixture of anxiety, incredulity and fear stormed through her. He wanted *her*? She could stay here for a couple of weeks, but even that wasn't in her plan. 'I can't leave my work—'

'You'd be surprised what you can do, Lily Kellaway, if the need and the motivation are there.' Unshakeable demand in each word, he continued. 'I want you to make my office run the way it has done for the past eleven years, with barely a hiccup to disturb me. When Maddie comes back, I want things to be so shipshape, she won't even know she's been gone.'

'Really. I'm sorry.' Lily had wanted a second chance, but not like this. She would make a fool of herself, would reveal her weaknesses in front of him. No. It was out of the question. As was explaining her reluctance to take up what he must see as a reasonable challenge. 'But I couldn't—'

'Yes, you could, and you will. You're the

right person to take it on, because you care enough about the outcome that you'll make sure it all works out.'

He didn't move, but she sensed the mental dusting of hands as he presented her with what he must view as a *fait accompli*. If he had any lingering concerns about feeling attracted to her, they were well buried.

Perhaps he had simply shut that attraction off? Not that she couldn't do the same. The stress of this situation had blurred her ability to act decisively, that was all.

He went on, his voice deepening with each word. 'I'm sure your organisational skills will be more than up to the task, and it's only a few months when all's said and done.'

'Only a f-few months.' He really wanted her to do this work herself. Had made his mind up and would refuse to accept anything else. As for her organisational skills, she choked back a bitter laugh. Lily organised her life to death, and it still wasn't enough.

The inescapability hit her. The notebook slipped from her fingers and fell to the floor. Pages fanned out like a startled lizard's ruffle. Her carefully controlled world fell on its ear at the same time.

With the addition of the month she had stupidly tossed in, it would be three months and three weeks. She couldn't afford to be here anywhere near that long.

She would have to prevaricate. Would have to accept his ultimatum for now, and convince him later to take Deb in her place.

'You don't have any choice, you know.' He retrieved her notebook and gently passed it to her.

The book was a symbol of her weakness, if he had but known it. Within its pages she attempted to maintain control of her life. Everything from shopping lists, to appointments, to work demands, to names of people she might need to call again.

'I've quite made up my mind, you see. So put your wonderful Deborah in charge of your agency. Let her do whatever it is you usually do.' His tone lowered to calm, focussed intent and he went on. 'And you, Lily Kellaway, give yourself to me.'

CHAPTER TWO

ZACHARY Swift had given Lily fifteen minutes to organise her agency matters. Lily's small electronic timer counted down the seconds even now. As a result, her phone conversation with Deborah was limited. It would help if she wasn't so aware of Zachary, seated in his office with the door open, working through twin mountains of paperwork with a determined diligence. She even liked that about him—drat the apparently hard-working man!

'I'll look after everything, Lily. Don't worry.' Deb's words barely registered.

It was difficult to notice anything but the man in her peripheral vision.

He glanced up as though sensing her gaze on him, and she felt heat warm her cheeks as she quickly looked away.

'Thanks, Deb.' Lily couldn't afford *not* to

take notice of this conversation. She jotted Deb's agreement to take over until further notice into her diary. 'You have the key to my office and the tapes…'

Where had Lily left the tapes? She couldn't visualise them. 'They should be beside the computer. If they're not, I might have left them in the top drawer of the desk. Re-direct the phone to your place. I'll call you tonight to catch up properly.'

The moment Lily ended the call, she scribbled self-help instructions on several sticky notes and slapped them into place above the phone, on the filing cabinet, over the dictation machine. She wished she could put up 'Don't be Aware of the Boss' notices, too.

And she was wasting mental energy when her fifteen minutes were almost up! She needed to take stock. Put steps in place to ensure she could emulate the operation here and seem reasonably competent during the standard 'unfamiliar territory' phase. But surely once things settled down a bit Zachary would be ready to take Deborah in her place?

'Do you have everything organised with your assistant, so you can focus solely on your work here from now on?' He stood in his office doorway, shirt sleeves rolled up, tie loosened.

What if she couldn't turn off the way she noticed him? What if this awareness of him didn't go away? Just kept increasing and deepening, as it was even now? 'Yes. It's all organised, although it involved a certain amount of reshuffling.'

She wished he would comb his ruffled, unruly hair. And, while he was at it, don the jacket he had removed the moment she'd agreed to his demand.

'I'm glad you're organised, because you'll need to be to do a good job here.' His mouth lifted at the corners as though to soften the challenging statement.

Why did he have to attract her, anyway? He was *so* not her type. If she ever took another man into her life—which was highly doubtful—he would be gentle, perhaps scholarly or poetic.

A man who would dress in twill trousers and misshapen pullover sweaters, not power business-suits of darkest grey that emphasised every muscle and sinew.

'I'll do the very best for you that I can, Mr Swift.' She deliberately avoided mentioning duration of time, and tried not to let anxiety get the better of her. She should be able to fool him long enough.

Her mentor at the institute might have said she should be open about her limitations, should tell people up front. But he didn't know what it was like to see the change in their faces, to read the pity, and worse, in their eyes.

And she would get over this mild, unexpected reaction to Zachary Swift. She would! She flipped her diary open and put it in a prominent place where she would be sure to see it at frequent intervals. 'I'll go through all this clutter, sort it out, and get to work on the most urgent of it.'

'Zach will do.' His hands rested loosely at his sides. 'And the clutter will have to wait a bit longer, I'm afraid.'

'If not this muddle…' She waved a hand. 'What do you want me to tackle first, exactly?'

'There's a group of proposals on tape on the desk somewhere that should have been done Friday.' He lifted a pile of papers as though to search for the tape, seemed to think better of it, and replaced them. 'Standard beginning for each one, but individualised for the last couple of pages. And a meeting scheduled for 12.30 today in the conference room for ten people, plus us.'

'No problem.' Just a heap of overdue proposals and a lunch meeting to prepare for all in the space of, oh, what—an hour and a half? Panic snapped at her heels, scrambled up her ankles and sank its claws into her calves. She swallowed hard, and forced a calm tone she didn't feel. 'I'll attend to typing the proposals. What's required for the meeting?'

'I'll want a copy of the proposals for each guest, plus one of each for myself. You'll also organise the meal, and take notes of anything pertinent said while we meet. Is that all clear?' He glanced up in time to catch her scribbling furiously into her notebook, and his face softened a little. 'You're certainly diligent, taking notes of everything…'

'It's the way I work.' She tipped her chin up and hoped he wouldn't question her about it. 'I'll get started straight away. If that's all for the moment?'

As soon as Lily said the words, she wanted to hyperventilate because she'd gone blank. She couldn't remember any of his instructions. Not a one. They'd fallen into one of those holes inside her head, and disappeared. If her notes didn't make sense once he turned his back, she was toast.

'That's all.' He started to turn away, and then stopped. For a moment he watched her, as though he wanted to puzzle her out. 'There are millions of dollars tied up in today's meeting. The largest project belongs to a man who can be difficult. I don't want him to have a reason to criticise my company.'

In other words, Lily had better not let Zach down! She focussed on breathing deeply in and out. 'I understand.'

He must have believed the act, because he gave a short, satisfied nod. 'I'll leave you to it. I trust I'll have the proposals very soon.' He walked into his office and shut the door.

Please let me get these things done in time. Lily re-read her notes. Fortunately, they made sense. Then she scribbled the meeting details onto the wall chart and into her diary, sticky-noted the need to find, type and collate the proposals, and dived for the phone book.

Thankfully she could cajole people when needed. That is, people other than the unshakeable Zachary Swift. Minutes later, with the meal agreed upon and delivery promised by 12.15 for a 12.30 start, she began to type.

The proposals were out, copied and onto Zach's desk with just minutes to spare. A convincing summation of several of Swift Enterprises' recent success stories, and individual offers to each company or business.

If his guests weren't duly impressed, well, Lily was. He dealt in *big* business. The knowledge of his prowess was quite…stimulating. *Intellectually.*

Even as she thought it, she studied his down-bent head from her vantage point in front of his desk, and acknowledged that no other male had appealed to her as much or as quickly as he had. What was wrong with her? Since moving to Sydney she had avoided even the slightest interest in men. It hadn't been difficult to make that choice until now.

'Good work.' Zach skimmed the final page of the last copy, and rose to his feet. 'Very accurate. Your typing speed must be as fast as your short—eh, note—taking.'

So he had noticed already that her code wasn't the usual shorthand script. If he asked, she would explain it as a newly developed recording style, which was nothing but the truth.

Sort of. But it worried her that he had picked up on that so quickly. What else might he see and wonder about?

When he stretched to relax his shoulders, she tried not to let her gaze be drawn to him. But she failed dismally. The man appeared to have some rather nice muscles under that suit, and something in her feminine make-up was attracted by that knowledge. In defence against her own thoughts, she crossed her arms.

'I'm glad you're happy with my work, although I know Deborah would have done just as well.' She had to get that in, the first building block towards her own imminent exit. 'These offers will mean a lot of new work, if they're all accepted.'

His gaze tracked over her hair, then her shoulders, before taking a leisurely path downward, and back up again. It was cold comfort to her to know that in this case, unlike when they'd discussed the Rochelle debacle, the attraction appeared to be mutual. She didn't *want* to want him, whether it was reciprocated or not.

He seemed to catch himself, and his glance shifted to the windows. 'Yes, but we're geared to handle that sort of influx. It's what my finance and planning gurus thrive on.'

His forehead creased in thought. 'This lot are an interesting mix of people. It's not always those in financial trouble who need a partner or to sell out. Two of them, for example, are estate inheritances.'

'Estate inheritances.' She repeated it while her fingers itched foolishly to smooth the attractive wrinkles from his brow. 'Stuck suddenly with a monstrosity they're not prepared to take on? Yes. I can understand why some people would simply want out. And you can make all these businesses profitable?'

He turned, his eyes lit with interest. 'I've already suggested other avenues for the ones that wouldn't have been.' Her temporary boss smiled, moved to sit on the edge of the desk, and leaned back just enough that she had a breathtaking view of the cleft of his chin and the long, tanned neck. 'You think like a businesswoman. I can see you're going to be even more of an asset than I'd hoped.'

'Well.' She tried to ignore the view, the elevation of her pulse. The warm feeling it gave her to receive his praise, however prosaic. She didn't plan on being here long enough for him to appreciate her very much! 'We'd best make our way to the conference room.'

'Let's hope they're all on time for the meeting. What did you choose for the food?' He rose, scooped up the pile of meeting notes and handed them to her.

Their fingers touched. Warmth. The slightest sandpapery feeling as his skin grazed hers. She experienced a swift, sharp wish to feel those fingers stroke her forehead, her jaw, her neck.

His gaze locked on her face, roved it, touched her eyes, nose, and lingered on her lips. 'Lily…'

'We…ah…' Her mouth dried. This was *not* anticipation, and he was *not* about to kiss her. For heaven's sake. When had she developed such an overactive imagination? She hurried into her office. Anything to gain a moment's reprieve.

And he had asked a question. The food! He had asked about the menu. The food…

Something good that would keep people happy.

That was all she could recall. So innovate, Lily! 'You'll like what I've chosen. Just wait and see.' There. Good enough, but she should have written the choices down as she'd agreed to them. 'I just need to get a couple of things and I'll be ready.'

'Good afternoon. It's a pleasure to meet you.' Lily's mellow words sounded calm. Unfazed. She looked completely relaxed as she worked to put their visitors at ease.

But Zach stood at her side at the entrance to the conference room and felt the tension that radiated from her. He nodded, smiled, shared a few words with each delegate, but he wasn't relaxed either. Wasn't calm. He hadn't been since that accidental touch as he'd handed her the approved proposals for this meeting, when a flood of heated response had rushed his system.

Indeed, he had wanted her from the moment they'd met, and he would be a fool to pretend otherwise. He might not like the knowledge, but he prided himself on facing the truth. Now he just had to find some way to overcome this unwelcome interest in her.

Since Lara had showed him five years ago what his life had to be, he had dated women casually. No friendships, no commitments, no compulsions driving his interest. He wasn't about to alter that credo. He couldn't.

But he and Lily stood so close now that they breathed the same air. And all he wanted was to snatch her up and get answers to the questions that pounded through his bloodstream. If he kissed her, would the lips that drew his gaze press in passion against his?

If he drew her close, would their bodies fit as though meant to be together? Would it feel right? Would desire flame in an instant, or ignite slowly? It was ridiculous. Too much. They had only just met, yet he couldn't seem to stop the distracting thoughts.

'Wallace. Please make yourself comfortable with the others.' He gestured towards the oval table laid for the upcoming meal, but part of his thoughts remained with the woman at his side.

She smelled of lily of the valley. Had she always worn her signature scent? He wanted to search out every pulse point and hidden place that carried it.

He suppressed a groan, and stuck out his hand as the final delegate arrived. 'Hardy. Welcome.'

'Am I?' Hardy gripped his hand with more force than was necessary. 'We'll soon see when I read the proposal you've concocted.' The man puffed out his ample girth. 'It had better impress me, or you can forget any chance of a sale. I'm only *considering* this move. Haven't decided yet.'

'Whatever decision you make will be respected.' But they both knew Hardy's trophy wife had run the company into the ground since he'd bought it for her.

'Hmph.' Andrew Hardy's gaze narrowed. 'Fashion can be a fickle business, might well turn around of its own accord before too long.'

'Anything's possible.' Zach tried not to show his disbelief.

When Hardy spotted Lily, his demeanour changed. Predatory interest rose in the florid face. 'And who might this beauty be?'

Mine. The thought was instantaneous. Unsettling. Possessive. Outrageous, because he and Lily had met only hours ago. 'Hardy, this is Lily Kellaway, my assistant. Lily, meet Andrew Hardy.'

The words fell from his mouth with bland disinterest. But his body growled, a rumble of warning deep within, and his gaze communicated that warning to Hardy. The man's eyes widened, then narrowed as he absorbed the silent message.

'Nice to meet you. I hope you enjoy your time with us today.' Lily's smile didn't reach her eyes. With her free hand, she pushed a folder towards the man's mid section.

The aggressive heat in Zach eddied away. She hadn't been taken in by Hardy's façade, had recognised something in the known womaniser that made her cautious.

'You'll find the proposal for your business in there.' Lily waggled the folder. 'You might care to take your seat and peruse it while lunch is being served.'

She was as cool as green salad. Zach suppressed a grin as Hardy stepped back to clasp the folder. A moment later, he had moved on.

They took their seats at the table. Lily sat at his right, and it felt as though she belonged there.

'Now that they're all seated, can you name them again for me, please?' She turned her face to his. 'Start with the person on my left and work your way around the table. Don't leave anyone out.' Her notebook rested on her knee, her pencil at the ready once again.

If he hadn't seen her hand clenched around that notebook, he wouldn't have known she was anything less than utterly confident. The knowledge that she was uneasy, a little uncertain, only made her more human in his eyes, more appealing.

Zach lowered his head to murmur the name

and a short description of the business of each person. She scribbled it all into her notebook, and nodded now and then to show she was keeping up.

He could brush her ear with his lips, and he doubted anyone would notice. His breath soughed across the object of his thoughts. She shivered, gave a soft gasp and looked up into his eyes.

So responsive. His gaze moved over the honey-gold hair, then shifted to her mouth, to kissable lips and a short, straight nose. To blue eyes the colour of deep tropical seas beneath a hot sun. Without conscious thought, he supplied the final name and relevant details.

She noted the information in her book, released her breath on a choppy sigh and leaned back. 'Thank you. That will make it easier to match up any comments I need to record.'

Did she know that her eyes took on a dreamy hue when she looked at him? Not avaricious or predatory, like Rochelle's, but something soft, almost vulnerable, and definitely sexy.

'Now, you wanted to know about the menu.' Lily's lashes fluttered as she whipped out a hand-written sheet of paper Zach had watched her garner from one of the waiting staff when she'd first entered the room. She dropped her gaze to the sheet. 'We discussed a few options, but what I chose in the end was seafood cups and mini beef-and-vegetable pies for starters…'

'Which gives us a chance to sample both red and white wines.' Zach no longer wanted to hear about the menu. He let his gaze linger on her. He wanted to kiss her instead.

She outlined the rest of the menu, and looked into his eyes. Warm spots of colour formed on her cheeks, but she only murmured, 'Your wine bill will be sky high. I thought you'd want the best.'

He dipped his head. 'Money is no object in this exercise.'

The guests perused their proposals while the meal was set out. Lively discussion ensued. Zach did his best to throw himself into it and put thoughts of Lily Kellaway's soft skin, and his desire to touch it, out of his mind.

'Once a proposal is accepted, it's handed to one of my team of experts.' He leaned forward as he explained the procedure to the man seated across the table from them. 'They either supervise the buy-out, or move straight in to manage the re-shaping if it's a share situation. No time is wasted. We're about making things work in the fastest, surest way we can.'

Over the entrées and a fine Sauvignon Blanc, Lily scribbled into her notebook, and picked at delicate prawns and Tasmanian scallops. Zach answered questions, parried comments and told himself he was doing well.

But all the while he was aware of her. In every break in discussions, his gaze went to her unerringly.

He looked at her now, and felt each bite of food she took explode on his own tongue, wanted to meld those tastes in exploration of her mouth. 'You chose the caterer well. Is it one I'd know?'

'Possibly not.' She glanced at the group discreetly situated at the far end of the room, then looked at him again. 'They—they're sort of like a galloping garçon. Zippy little van, go anywhere in a hurry. Several local offices have used them.'

'And you know this because you phoned other secretaries, rather than going at it blind and ringing restaurants and caterers first. Clever.'

Clever, determined, so eager to do her work

well, that he couldn't stop himself from wondering if she'd be equally as enthusiastic and unwavering about pleasing a man under the enveloping cloak of a long, sensual night. It wasn't a question he should be considering.

But his praise brought her gaze back to his face with startled gratitude.

'I have to— I try to think outside the box.' She made it sound like an impediment, and hurriedly took a taste of saffron-rice paella, closing her eyes to savour the sharp, tangy fragrance and taste.

Despite his best intentions, his lids drooped as he watched her enjoy the food.

'Mmm.' She glanced at her plate. 'I have to admit, this is very pleasant.'

He ate *salade de boeuf* with buttermilk mash, and noted the fineness of her bone structure, the delicate shoulders beneath the blazer. His body twitched. Yes, this was pleasant—in a torturous sort of way.

Her attention focussed on him. The colour in her face deepened, and she looked quickly away again.

'You've done a good job with the lunch, Lily.' He tried to bring his thoughts back to business. Was it to be like this any time they got closer than the width of a desk away from each other? 'If the rest of your work for me is equally as professional and useful, I'll be very pleased, indeed.'

She straightened in her chair, primmed her mouth and clutched at her notebook again. 'You can rely on Best Secretarial Agency to take care of your business needs. You won't be let down again.'

When the desserts arrived, conversation lulled in favour of enjoyment of the delicate fare. Lily relaxed, let go of the deathly grip on her notebook and turned her attention to her food.

Instead of relaxing with her, Zach's tension increased. *Why* hadn't he been able to banish personal thoughts of her from his mind?

Maybe it wasn't his mind that was causing the problem. Maybe he needed to indulge his curiosity. He twirled the stem of his wine glass between his fingers. One little taste test. Just to see. So he could put it out of his thoughts once and for all…

'The coffee crème is delicious.' She turned to him and smiled. A simple smile, yet he wanted to rush her into the supply closet at the rear of the conference room and kiss her among the broom sticks, buckets and mops.

He was losing his mind. Could only think of tasting *her*, nothing else, even though every fibre in his being warned him it was dangerous to think this way. Even for a moment. 'Um—'

'I hope the lemon panna cotta and fruit coulis equals it.' She dipped her spoon into the confection again. 'Would you like me to ask the caterers to give you a serving of the coffee crème, too? I'm sure they'd have some spares, if you'd like to try both.'

'No. Thank you.' He cleared his throat, forced civil words out, couldn't quite hide the deeper timbre of his voice. 'I'll be fine with… what I have.'

He tried his lemon panna cotta, praised her choice and tried not to think about her mouth. They were in the middle of a conference meeting, and his awareness of her was off the scale.

She blinked. That rapid flutter again of her lashes. 'That's very good. I'm glad you're enjoying your… dessert.'

'Yes.' The coffee arrived. With relief, he turned to the man on his right and engaged him in conversation until things began to wind down.

Finally, the time came to deliver his short

closing speech. He got to his feet. 'You'll all need time to think, to confer with colleagues, to run the figures. I suggest phone conferences tomorrow and Wednesday to conclude our business. Phone Lily in the morning. She'll let you know what time slots are available.'

From the corner of his eye, he saw Lily scribble something in her notebook and underline it.

With murmured thanks, the guests moved out. Zach saw them off at the door while Lily set the caterers to work on the clean up. She returned to his side just as Hardy clamped an unlit cigar into his mouth and said around it, 'A phone conference doesn't suit me. Come to my office tomorrow at 4.00 p.m. I'll give you my answer then.'

'I'm not available at that time.' Zach tried to instil regret into his tone. 'Nor will I be available for anything but phone conferences for the rest of the week. You'll understand that I'm busy.'

As a concession, Zach acknowledged the other man's probable commitments. 'I'm sure you must have a full schedule, too. Perhaps you'd like to call on Thursday or Friday. I'm prepared to extend the deadline for you.'

'We'll see.' Hardy barged out the door, proposal tucked beneath his arm and a scowl on his face.

'Nice exit.' Lily's chuckle washed over Zach, sensual and free. She looked into his eyes, the smile still lingering on her lips. 'Do you think he'll accept your proposal?'

'I expect he will, eventually.' He dipped his head closer to her face. Wanted her. Didn't want to.

She gasped. A soft sigh of sound that revealed her reaction to him. 'Well, um, I'll just have one last word with the caterers, then. To make sure they're, um, all finished catering.'

'Don't wait for me. You go on back.' She drew in a shaky breath. 'I'll join you when I've calmed—in a minute. *I'll join you in a minute.*'

He left. It was either that or snatch her into his arms and kiss them both senseless, momentary acquaintances or not.

CHAPTER THREE

'CAN I help you?' Lily closed the filing-cabinet drawer, and offered a questioning smile to the boy who stood in school uniform in the middle of the reception area of her office, his shoulders hunched, his profile to her.

Two and a half weeks had passed since she'd started work at Swift Enterprises. Two and a half weeks filled with a growing, unspoken awareness between her and a man unlike any she had known.

Clients had come and gone. Lily had managed the appointments, ploughed through the pile-up of work, and hadn't bungled anything too badly. Earlier today, Hardy had finally signed on the dotted line, yielding to what he knew was a great deal, just as Zach had predicted he would.

Lots of things had happened, but this was

the first time Lily had seen a child in the offices. The boy should have seemed out of place, yet somehow he didn't.

'Oh, hi. I didn't see you there. Is Zach ready?' He turned fully to face her, slung his backpack onto one of the chairs and pushed his hands into his pockets in a gesture she had seen Zach use countless times. 'He said we'd have to go by four o'clock.'

'And it's almost that now, isn't it?' Slowly, she returned to her desk as she tried to assimilate what she was seeing. This boy was the image of the man on the other side of the closed office door. The same thick-fringed hazel eyes, same hair. Same mannerisms, same frown. Everything. It was all there.

Zach's son?

The possibility hadn't occurred to her until now. Faced with it, she felt…unnerved. Her mind leapt immediately ahead. Where was the mother of this child? What relationship did Zach have with her? Why didn't the boy call his father 'Dad'?

And what game had Zach been playing with *her*? He was a well-known and, it was assumed, *carefree* bachelor, and had been sending out 'attracted to you' signals since they'd met. Those signals had only grown stronger on both sides, she had thought, even though Zach had been clearly fighting them all the way.

She'd had no intention of acting on them, either, of course. Had intended to put a stop to her side of things just as soon as she worked out how. Hadn't she?

Of course she had! But what had Zach been thinking?

'Um, your fath— Mr Swift—is taking a phone call.' The boy shouldn't be made uncomfortable because of her surprise and shock. And she *was* shocked. 'I'm sure he'll be finished his call in a moment.'

The boy nodded. 'I'll just wait, then.'

'Yes. Make yourself at home.' She pretended to go back to work, but all that showed up on her screen as she typed was meaningless gibberish.

At times recently, she had wanted to yield to Zach's interest, and to her own. To step forward instead of stepping back, just once, and see what happened. She shouldn't have wanted that. She was living a deception. He wouldn't want her if he knew her secrets, and she needed to protect herself, too.

But it appeared he also had secrets.

Zach opened his door and came out. He glanced at her, and his eyes flared with familiar heat.

Then he turned and spotted the boy. His face softened in affection and pride. In two strides, he had the young man in a headlock, ruffling his hair as he hugged him close. 'Dan. Good lad, you're right on time. You didn't have any trouble with the buses?'

The boy wrapped wiry arms around the man, pushed his head into his chest and put all his effort into getting loose. He grinned when he broke free. 'Nope. I'm ready to go. You're getting weaker, you know. You barely held me that time.'

A bittersweet smile touched Zach's face. 'You're the one getting stronger. You're growing up too fast.'

Zach made a show of getting his briefcase, but Lily saw the tenderness he tried to hide and, despite her confusion, her heart softened. Zach clearly loved this child.

He rattled off a few instructions to her before he turned back to Daniel. 'Did you two meet? This is Lily. She's filling in while Maddie is away. The other secretary...' he cleared his throat '…didn't work out, so Lily has taken over.'

Lily finished jotting his instructions into her diary. She closed it and looked at the boy. 'Hello again.'

'I'm Daniel.' He shook her hand, mumbled, 'You're prettier than the last one,' and turned a little red in the face. 'I mean—'

'Thank you.' She turned back to her desk to save him from further embarrassment. And to avoid having to look at Zach. 'I won't keep you both. You clearly have somewhere you need to be.'

A slight frown between his brows, Zach nodded. Then the boy drew his attention.

'Mum said you're invited to dinner again tonight, if you want. She's running errands this afternoon, but she'll bring home something nice.' Daniel gathered his school bag and slipped it over his shoulders. He gave Zach a bit of a glare. 'I could go to the orthodontist by myself, you know. If I can manage a couple of buses, I can manage—'

'All the buses. Yes, but I promised when you first got the braces on that I'd take you to every appointment.' Zach ruffled the dark hair again. 'And I always—'

'Keep your promises, I know. But I'm not a baby. You don't need to mollycoddle me.' The boy sighed, and made for the door.

Lily watched him, and tried to contain the anger and dismay that had filled her at Daniel's innocent words. Zach was still involved with the mother of his child! He had been toying with Lily. She felt stupid for not having realised his interest wasn't sincere. Felt second-rate, as she had when Richard had ended their engagement.

'I'm not mollycoddling.' Zach waved Daniel off. 'Go on ahead. I'll catch up with you at the elevators.'

As the boy left, Zach turned back into the room. 'Is everything all right? You seem agitated.' A rather ferocious expression closed in on his face, and he said without any inflection at all, 'Don't you like children?'

'No, it's not that. Everything's fine.' His protectiveness of the boy made Lily ache for things she didn't have, for family to stand by her. But it didn't change the fact that Zach was now clearly and utterly out of bounds to her. And, right now, she really didn't like him very much. At all!

She busied herself putting a dictation tape

into the machine, fiddled with the wishbone earpieces, then placed her hands in readiness against the keyboard. As she did so, she realised the child's name had slipped from her memory. She sought for it, but didn't find it. Darn it! 'It was nice to meet your son, but shouldn't you be going?'

'Ah.' His eyes narrowed as he studied her. 'I think you've just explained the sudden chill in the air. If there's a child, there's got to be a mother, and therefore—'

'You're having dinner with that mother. You're clearly very close.' Oh, couldn't he just go? She didn't want to have this discussion. 'It's got nothing to do with me.'

'Hasn't it? You and I have been—'

'Hurry up, old man. We'll be late!' The warning floated down the corridor, affection wrapped up in the cheeky words. A moment later, the boy poked his head back into the room. 'Are we leaving some time this millennium, or what?'

Zach hesitated, gritted his teeth and strode to join the boy. 'Yes, Daniel. We're leaving. Let's go.'

Daniel, Daniel, Daniel. His name is Daniel. Lily pretended not to watch their exit. As soon as they left, she wrote the boy's name down, although she suspected it would now stick firm for her. Usually, if she could get a piece of information beyond that short-term memory area, it stayed with her for good.

An hour later, after swinging from chagrin to anger and back again, she was doing her best to force Zach Swift out of her mind. She would go on doing that until she crushed every memory of the attraction she had experienced towards him. Utter rejection should have been her response from the start.

As she began to pack up her desk, a middle-aged woman stepped into the room. 'I hope I didn't startle you, dear. Are you about to leave?'

'Hello. Yes, it's almost closing time, but is there some way I can help you?' Lily pushed the last of the folders into the drawer and gave the woman her full attention.

'There is, I hope, but this isn't really a business matter.' The lady smiled. 'Let me introduce myself. I'm Anne Swift, Zach's mother.' She stuck out a hand.

Lily snatched up a sticky notepad and scribbled 'Anne Swift' onto it, then took the other woman's hand and looked into kindly yellow-green eyes. She couldn't help returning the warm smile she found there, even as her picture of Zach shifted for the second time this afternoon.

She had assumed he had no family at all. That he lived for his company, utterly focussed on making money. Lily had even felt a connection, because she didn't have any significant family ties either. Not any more.

Within the space of an hour, Zach had a son, a mother of that son, and a mother of his own.

'I'm afraid Zach's not in. He took Daniel to an orthodontist appointment.' *And, later, he's going to have dinner with the mother of his child. They'll probably make love once Daniel's asleep.*

'Just as I hoped. I timed it so he would be gone when I got here.' A warm chuckle erupted from the small, well-rounded frame. 'Now, I know you're just new, dear, but I need you to join me in a teensy-tiny conspiracy against my darling son.'

Well, that sounded interesting, if rather dangerous! Why would Zach's mother want to conspire against him? 'I'm not quite sure I can help you…'

'You can, and it will be for his own good.' Anne gave her merry laugh again. 'I just need to explain. Come to coffee with me?'

* * *

The next morning, Zach greeted Lily with a watchful expression. Lily didn't know what to think. During their stop for coffee, Anne Swift hadn't mentioned anyone special in Zach's life. But, then, Zach's mother had been focussed on other things and perhaps had seen no reason to say anything.

I hope Anne enjoyed her meal, anyway.

The older lady had bought enough take-out containers of food during that jaunt for coffee to supply several hungry eaters. Perhaps she froze portions for herself. Or maybe she had invited guests that night.

'Re-direct the phones. We'll go to lunch early.' Zach spoke in a silken tone from his position in the doorway that connected their two offices. His words made her jump, because for once she'd had no clue of his nearness.

He shifted his stance slightly. 'There's a pub not far from here that serves good, fresh battered fish and chips.'

'I can't.' Lily didn't quite meet his gaze, stared instead at a spot on the wall behind him. *I won't make myself vulnerable to you by getting too close.* 'I'm busy.'

'Let me make this clearer. It's not an invitation, Lily.' He looked down his nose at her, let her see the glitter of anger and frustration for a moment in his eyes before he hooded them. 'Your presence is required.'

Maybe this wasn't personal. Maybe she had done something, made some mistake here in the office?

Her mind raced with possibilities. She'd been skirting around him since she got here this morning. Had that made her lax in her duties somehow? Or had her shortcomings found her out?

Zach hustled her out of the office while she was still worrying. He rattled off their order to the bistro lady at the pub without consulting Lily for her choice, then led Lily to their allocated table and proceeded to drum his fingers on the polished surface.

'What if I hadn't wanted whiting fillets?' She took the paper serviette from around her cutlery, and set everything just so in front of her. It might not be smart to goad him, yet she couldn't help herself. 'I might have preferred the roast pork, or the chicken pot-pie.'

His fingers came to an abrupt stop. He said, apparently out of nowhere, 'Did you know that Daniel loves fish and chips?'

'Does he?' She kept her voice neutral, but

wondered about that smooth-as-glass tone of his. 'That's nice.'

Their meals and drinks arrived. He held her gaze over the rim of his beer glass until they were alone again. 'Daniel and I live just around the corner from each other. He stays overnight with me often, drops in evenings and weekends during the day. It's pretty much open house to him any time I'm home.'

What about Zach staying the night with Daniel's mother, or vice versa? Not that Lily cared about his bed partners, she told herself fiercely. And he was baiting her right now. She was sure of it. She glared at him, and took a defiant sip of her lemon squash.

Not another word would pass her lips on the topic. If he had something to say, then let him say it.

After eating most of the meal in loaded silence, she began to toy with her half-empty sachet of tartare sauce. Anything to keep her gaze from his, really, but in the end she couldn't help it. Her resolve teetered, and fell. 'You mentioned Daniel. What about his mother? What's her name?'

'His mother is the same one I have, actually. I wondered how long it would take you to ask.'

He speared a chip with his fork, seemed to take delight in the aggressive movement. 'Our mother is Anne. Anne Swift.'

While he ate the chip, Lily drew a deep breath of pub-laden air and tried to assimilate this news. Zach and Daniel were brothers. There *was* no woman with a long history of involvement with Zach. Lily had jumped to a massive conclusion.

Her heart began to beat out an uneasy, rapid rhythm. 'But that's not, that can't be—'

'Daniel was a change-of-life baby, conceived three months before our father died.' He laid down his cutlery, drew two well-thumbed photos from his wallet and flipped them one after the other across the table to her.

'The first is of me and my parents the year before Dad died. It was an aneurysm.' He spoke without particular inflection, but his fingers clenched. 'He didn't suffer. It was very fast.'

'I'm so sorry.' She suppressed the urge to touch his hand, and repeated the information over in her head because she couldn't bear it if she were to forget this later. At times like this she hated her impediment!

'I miss him.' The understatement somehow

made Zach's loss all the more real to her. His gaze dropped to the other photo. 'The second is Mum, Daniel and me. It was taken last year when we visited the Imax theatre here in Sydney for a treat for Dan's birthday.'

'In the first, you look about eighteen.' He looked young and happy, as Lily had felt before her accident. She was still happy, she told herself, but for ever changed, just as Zach must have been by his father's death.

But Zach hadn't started this conversation to elicit sympathy. He had wanted to confront her mistake, to make a point about her jumping to conclusions. That was clear to her, and not entirely fair. 'Why didn't you say something when I—?'

'Drew that conclusion with no help from me? By the time I realised what you thought, Dan had interrupted and I had to go.' He reached for the photos. Their fingers touched, and he kept his grip on hers. 'And then I wondered if it might be best to let you believe it.'

Anger gave way to something different. Something deeper. She sought the answer in his eyes, and found a wary, reluctant awareness that echoed deep inside her.

'Yet you've told me. What changed your

mind?' She pulled her hand free, and hoped he couldn't see how much she had wanted to leave it in his grasp.

'Honesty.' His gaze remained steadfastly on hers. 'I don't like deceptions.'

Deceptions such as secretaries not confessing their limitations to their boss, and planning to get out of working for him, even though he'd insisted on it? But her situation was different.

His body tensed as he studied her. 'I couldn't let you believe I was committed to some phantom woman. But you and I have been aware of each other, and it's best if you know that I'm not willing to get involved with you.'

'You don't want a relationship?' He had some nerve, making these assumptions, when all she had done was reciprocate his own interest. 'What makes you think I would want to get involved, either? I don't want *any* kind of entanglement!'

His mouth pulled into a scowling line. 'I tried commitment once, Lily. What I had to offer wasn't enough. I had to let it go.'

'You'd have a lot in common with my ex-fiancé, then.' Her words came, uncensored, straight from the hurt she'd been through. 'It turned out he couldn't cope with commitment, either. That experience pretty much cured me where men and relationships are concerned.'

His gaze whipped to her eyes. 'I didn't know you'd been engaged. Perhaps you and I have more in common than you think.' His mouth turned down, as though his thoughts weren't happy ones. 'I was engaged once, too, five years ago. When my fiancée needed things from me that I couldn't give her, we both got hurt. That experience made me accept my limitations. I can't give a woman more than a token, fleeting interest.'

Just for a moment, Lily almost felt that his eyes asked for understanding, that she saw regret in the hazel depths.

'There are things in my life that just make it impossible for me to give more. To have—' He dropped his gaze abruptly to the table top. When he lifted it again, his face was a strong mask, etched in determination. 'I wouldn't change anything.'

If anything, his expression became fiercer. 'I'm not willing to find myself backed into a corner by a relationship with a woman again, that's all!'

Well, she didn't want those feelings, either.

She didn't welcome them any more than he did.

'You speak as though there's a risk we might actually get entangled.' They shared an awareness and interest. Strong, yes, but not impossible to overcome. 'But we're quite safe. Neither of us wants this. We certainly don't have to act on it.'

She forced a smile. 'Those sparks in the air have been hanging around, it's true, but, now we've talked about it, we can put it behind us and get on with a proper, uncomplicated working relationship until I leave—for as long as it's needed.'

With a determined toss of her head, she rose. 'Shall we go back to work?'

'Just like that, and it's gone and we forget it was ever there?' He gave a humourless laugh, put the photos away and got to his feet, too.

'Yes. Just like that.' She hurried through the bar and out onto the street, and hoped her words would prove to be true. If they didn't, she was in big trouble.

CHAPTER FOUR

NOTHING was ever easy. Lily twisted the straps of her 1968 hand-beaded bag—Australian eBay, $2.95 plus postage—in her lap and just knew this whole thing was a big mistake. It was Friday evening, the official end of her working week. She should have been at home resting up with a favourite DVD movie. Or out with the girls, having a bit of uncomplicated fun.

She glanced at the man seated in the rear of the taxi beside her. Tonight, in evening clothes, Zach looked as though he could take on the whole world and win.

Dark trousers hugged his strong thighs. A matching jacket rested casually over the crook of one arm. The formal shirt, pristine white, pleated, and such an exact fit that it was probably custom-made, accentuated the broad chest and shoulders.

Against her will, she wanted to touch him. To feel whether his body was as firm and solid as it looked, wanted to embrace his power.

Lily should never have agreed to this. It was the baklava. Anne Swift had led her into temptation with food for the gods at that Greek restaurant right near Zach's office building. Then, when Lily's guard was down—and she'd been on a nice sugar buzz and had taken her first sip of the best flat black ever—*bam*, Anne had gone in for the kill.

Anne had had a persuasive way about her, but what did Lily know about families doing well-intentioned things to make each other happy? She should be focussing on not wanting Zach!

The taxi turned a corner. Her thigh bumped against his leg. She drew a sharp breath.

'He probably hates surprises,' she mumbled towards the window.

I do not want to say Happy Birthday and brush my lips against his cheek. I do not want to be here, at all!

But Lily had agreed to schedule and attend this 'business meeting' tonight as a ruse to get Zach here for the surprise his mother had taken such trouble to plan.

'Would you please face me, not the window, if you insist on muttering? At least give me the chance to try to lip read.' Zach's voice rumbled with something just dark enough to facilitate a fresh batch of shivers down the length of her spine.

The same dark something she had seen when she'd emerged from their office cloakroom dressed for the evening. There hadn't been time to go home to change. They had left straight from work, but not before he'd seared her with just the same look she was receiving now.

She cast about for some excuse for her mumbling, for some distraction from her awareness of him. Their arrival at the exclusive harbour-side address saved her.

The Opera House shimmered in the distance. Cars crawled like busy, multi-coloured ants across the harbour bridge. Boats of all shapes and sizes dotted the water.

It was beautiful, sultry, a living, breathing part of the city that couldn't help but entice. At another time, her surroundings would have worked wonders on her mood. 'We're here. And right on time to see your *client*—Mr Goodman. For the *business discussions* he scheduled.'

Oh, she had worked hard to make sure she retained this name and the business-meeting ruse that went with it!

Zach wondered why Lily's voice had been breathless, and sounded patently relieved. Not to mention her emphasising half her words as though she believed he had suddenly lost most of his comprehension skills. 'It's a coincidence that Vince chose this venue. I'm a part owner,' Zach replied.

Was she relieved because they could finally quit the confines of the rear seat of the taxi? Because they wouldn't have to be in such close proximity any longer? Was she as sensually charged with awareness of him as he was of her at this moment?

So much for her idea that they could bury their attraction to each other.

Lily nodded with what seemed to be unnecessary enthusiasm. 'Yes, your moth—that is, *Mr Goodman* mentioned you were a part owner in the restaurant.'

'The owner had allowed the place to lose its verve. He didn't want to sell out, so I bought a share, helped him improve the appeal to the public.' He didn't care about that, only wanted to thread his fingers into her upswept hair, to touch her scalp and feel it tighten beneath his hands.

She wasn't right for him. More to the point, he could never be right for her. The woman had a cat and some sort of egg-producing fowl, for heaven's sake. Five years ago, he hadn't even been able to meet Lara's demands. And his ex-fiancée's idea of home-making had been to take a page from *Homes of the Rich and Beautiful* and have a team of decorators apply it to her apartment.

Zach paid the driver, and helped Lily out of the taxi. Got distracted by a glimpse of long leg beneath the shimmering dress.

'You look sensational tonight.' He growled the words from deep within. 'You might as well know, I want to examine every part of you. At my leisure, and preferably in private.'

'It's—you can't simply up and say—' She sputtered to a stop, but twin flags of colour flared in her cheeks and her eyes glittered.

'Then I'll just look.' He did exactly that, taking his time to examine every inch of her. The dress was a shimmering blend of autumn shades that shaped to her torso and hips, and flared just enough from knee to ankle to make movement possible, with a slit that ended mid-thigh.

High in front, a small V-dip in the back, it was perfectly respectable and rather old-worldly. But it caressed her in ways that made his hands itch to do likewise.

'Dressed as you are, and with your hair piled up so that your neck seems smooth and endless, is it any surprise that I want to draw you back into the cab and kiss you until we both run out of breath?'

'You have a b-business meeting,' she stammered, and clutched her evening bag in both hands as though to shield herself from him.

Or maybe to stop those hands from doing something they shouldn't—like reaching out to him? Their gazes clashed, and he saw the trammelled awareness in her eyes, and wanted to tell her to let it go free, to let it lead her…to him.

It was madness. But maybe it would happen, be unleashed, before either of them would be able to move beyond it.

For surely, if they gave in to this mutual interest, the results would be less than he imagined. It couldn't possibly be all that his body and his senses told him he could find with her. 'We need to deal with this, Lily. Because it's pretty clear it won't deal with itself.'

'We can't. We've already agreed neither one of us wants any type of relationship.' She took several hasty steps away from him. 'We need to go in now. We don't want to keep your associate waiting.'

'We'll go in, but this isn't resolved.' He yielded for the moment, but he made no attempt to shield her from the purpose in his gaze. There *would* be a reckoning of some sort, and it would be soon. 'I still don't see why Goodman couldn't have seen me during the day.'

The man was an acquaintance of his mother. He and Zach had done business before. Across a desk in broad daylight. It was Zach's thirtieth birthday today, and, although he admitted that the sight of Lily in a clingy dress was a nice gift, he could think of things he would rather have done with his evening.

Like take Lily somewhere secluded and let nature have its way with both of them...

'Mr Goodman must have been busy during the day, I suppose. Let's go. It's, er, this way, by the look of it.' Lily gave him one short, agitated glance, then turned and hurried towards the entrance to the building.

She had freckles dotted across the milky satin of her shoulders. Freckles that seemed to invite him to lean closer, to press his lips to each little dot, to taste the freshness of soft, sweet skin.

Zach groaned, and to cover the sound broke into speech. 'Have you been here before? You seem to know exactly where you're going.'

His formal clothing was strangling him. The need to touch Lily was strangling him. Just a couple of short steps and he could have her in his arms.

'I haven't been here before, but I've heard the views from the restaurant floor are spectacular.' Lily pushed the door open and stepped inside.

When they left the elevator on the top floor, the owner himself met them. He whisked them towards a set of concertina doors without giving Zach a chance to even enquire after the business.

'It appears you're headed for the function room.' Zach wondered at the very obvious mistake, and at the man's sense of suppressed urgency. 'We're to meet someone in the restaurant itself—'

Without responding, the owner flung the doors open.

'Happy Birthday!'

'Surprise!'

The room erupted with noise and cheers.

'I've been had.' Zach turned and drew Lily to his side. A brand of ownership? A promise that their shared attraction *would* be addressed? He didn't know, knew only that it was right for his fingers to wrap around Lily's arm as he took in his mother's wide smile, Daniel's grin, and the sea of familiar faces.

Wall-to-floor panes of glass beyond them revealed the harbour in all its splendour. The magnificence of it shone for a moment in Lily's eyes. He could drown in her. Too easily.

The restaurant owner stepped forward, grinning, and offered a hearty handshake. 'It's too long since you've visited your investment. Enjoy your night.'

Then his mother gave him a quick, one-armed hug. 'Happy Birthday, darling. Are you utterly surprised? Vince thought it a great lark. He *does* have a business proposition to discuss, but Lily has booked an appointment.'

'I didn't suspect at all.' His focus on Lily had dulled his awareness of other things. Even now, the feel of her arm beneath his fingers tantalised him.

When had his mother approached Lily about tonight? All Zach had known was Goodman's demand for a dinner meeting. Complete with secretary to take urgent and important notes!

He turned to look at her again. The results of his hold on her carried a slow burn through his system. 'But I think my new secretary probably has a few things to answer for.'

She dutifully laughed, but for a moment her eyes held a stark vulnerability. Why? He didn't know, but he wanted to take that pain from her. A wave of protectiveness and possessiveness washed over him.

He didn't consider how his actions might look to the many people who observed them. He just reached for her and accepted this had to happen. 'I think you owe me a birthday salute, at the least, for tricking me this way.' What harm could it do to kiss her here, in a crowded room?

She stiffened at his side. 'Oh, no, I don't think it would be a good idea.'

'I do.' He settled his mouth on hers without giving her a chance to protest further. Without giving himself time to think about it any more, either. Cupped her face in his hands, and tasted the soft fullness of her lips beneath his.

That was all he intended. A simple taste. A chance to prove this wasn't so amazing. That he could walk away and not regret it. But she melted into him, into their kiss.

And he fell into a fathomless ocean of sensation and feeling. Her hands on his forearms, burning through the cloth of his coat. The soft, blurry fragrance of her perfume filling him as he breathed her in. Her mouth moving with his as though they'd always been together.

A feeling of such rightness and of emptiness finally being filled swept over him. He held back a gasp. It took all his will not to drag her in until their bodies melded utterly and he forgot everything. All he had proved was how right they were with each other, and he didn't know what to do about that.

He forced his hands to relax their grip on her arms. His mouth to take one last, lingering taste, then disengage.

The silence immediately near them filled suddenly with chatter and laughter. He didn't know if talk had actually stopped, or he just hadn't been able to hear it while she'd been in his arms.

'You shouldn't have done that.' She whispered the reprimand. Her flushed face revealed the same shock he felt.

The slight puffiness of lips well kissed

wrenched a gasp from deep inside him—he held it back, but could do nothing about the gaze that caressed her from head to toe.

'Happy Birthday, Zach.' She pinned on a tremulous smile that might have been meant to convince onlookers that the kiss had been a casual salutation.

Would they believe her? Or would they perceive the depths of the exchange in the same way he had experienced those depths just now?

Lily took a shaky step away from Zach, then another. 'I hope you enjoy your…celebration.'

All Lily wanted to do was to back away and keep on going. Her heart pounded, her hands shook.

Zach had kissed her in front of a room full of people. Had touched her and drawn a response she'd thought had died the day Richard Pearce had abandoned her to a hospital ward, and a future he no longer wanted to share.

No. That wasn't right. She had *never* felt this way. Not with Richard. Not with any man. Did the people around them know it? Could they see Zach had unlocked something inside of her that could carry her away? Make her ignore everything that mattered?

Anne Swift caught her hand in hers and gave it a squeeze. 'Thank you so much for your help. I couldn't have pulled this off without you.'

Her friendliness and the absence of any kind of surprise or dismay gave Lily hope that the kiss *hadn't* revealed as much to others as she had thought it might have.

Anne turned slightly to include someone standing at her side. 'You've met my second son, I think?'

'Yes.' Lily offered the boy a smile. She hoped it looked genuine, because she regretted her impulsive thoughts the last time she'd seen him. 'Daniel and I met at the office.'

'And how are you enjoying the job?' Anne asked. 'Was it difficult to come in part-way through and take over from, oh, what was her name?' She laughed, and waved a dismissing hand. 'My memory isn't what it used to be.'

Lily bit down on a half-hysterical laugh. *Tell me about it!*

'Her name was Rochelle.' Lily tried not to go sour-faced at the name. 'And I'm only filling in for a short time at your son's office.'

'You're filling in for the length of our agreement, so quite a bit longer yet.' Zach spoke right beside her. 'You're mine for that time, Lily, and I plan to hold you to every one of the agreed days.'

'Well, I've done my best to get things in order in the office.' She forced herself to treat his statement at face value, but her skin prickled as she absorbed his quiet words, and their double-edged meaning.

He couldn't mean to pursue their attraction further? The one kiss had been devastation enough.

She had to get out of this man's orbit. The sooner, the better. 'I'm sure any of my staff would be able to take over and keep things going quite seamlessly from this point.' If she could bring Deborah in…

His instant, narrowed gaze bored through her. 'But that's not going to happen, my dear. Now, let's go mix with the crowd. I'm sure lots of these people would like to meet you.'

My dear. Oh, it had been nothing but a throwaway line. Yet, even as she told herself this, she reacted to the heat of awareness in his gaze.

'I was about to leave, actually. This is your night. The business dinner was just a ruse to get you here. You don't need me hanging around.'

'Nonsense. If you think I'll let you go now…' A certain tautness of his features made his determination clear. 'Besides, a lot of these people are business contacts. You might pick up some interest in your agency. That's what you want, isn't it? To build up business?'

'Naturally, I do.' She couldn't very well say anything else. 'But I can't push my agency down people's throats at your party.'

He took her hand and tucked it through the crook of his elbow. 'You could if you wanted to. But, if not, then just enjoy yourself and don't be a drama queen about it, there's a good girl.'

Ooh! While she was struggling to overcome her flash of ire, he excused them to his mother and brother and started around the room, introducing her to uncles, aunts and cousins, and more business colleagues than she could count. She would never remember most of them.

And Zach still wasn't willing to let her bring in a replacement for herself. What would she do?

'You seem to have quite a few relatives. I'm surprised at how many have travelled to be here.' That made it sound as though Zach wasn't worth making the trip for, and this wasn't *her* family they were talking about.

'Sorry. That came out all wrong. Why don't I go mingle for a while by myself?' she suggested rather desperately. 'Let you get on with enjoying your guests?'

'Why not stay with me? I'm enjoying your company, and it's my birthday. Don't you want to keep me happy?' Aside from the hand that tucked her against his side, he didn't touch her. But his glance held heat.

'I shouldn't.' But she stayed. She was too weak to say no again and walk away. And she convinced herself it would be fine. They'd shared a kiss. But, when his common sense returned, he would have no desire to repeat it. Why would he?

They ate sumptuous finger food passed around by discreet waiters, and more food piled onto a groaning buffet table. During the informal toasts there were a lot of jokes about football. Perhaps Zach had played in high school or something. He certainly had lovely shoulders for the game.

When Zach spoke, she was thinking about those shoulders bared and raised above her. Stark, illicit thoughts that shocked and enthralled at once.

'Come dance with me.'

'You should dance with some of your guests.' Her voice sounded almost normal. She hoped he couldn't see the desperation and lingering desire for him in her gaze.

She couldn't dance with him. Couldn't be held close against the solid wall of his chest without revealing just how much she wanted to be that close, and stay that way for as long as she possibly could.

Darkness had set in. The harbour outside sparkled with twinkling lights. There was far too much of the fairy tale about this night already for her to risk a dance with the prince of the evening.

'I'd rather dance with you.' Before she could argue, he led her onto the dance floor.

She belatedly realised that she had imagined something quite different to the reality. All over the floor, people were grooving down to a fast-paced song from a 1980's movie. This would be no smoochy, mouth-watering moment, and she felt momentarily chagrined by the turn of her thoughts.

Yet the dance moves, that felt natural in the privacy of her living room or when she went out with the girls to a club, seemed quite different with Zach's gaze locked on her.

Every move she made felt sensually charged. Every move *he* made seemed designed to make her more aware of him. Nobody around them was taking the slightest bit of notice, yet she felt so conscious of the tension between them that it was a physical sharpening down her spine.

And he felt it, too, all of it. She knew it, because he didn't bother to hide the heat in his eyes when their gazes locked. That blatant barrage of sensual interest stole her breath.

Almost at the end of the number, he moved close, his hands firm on the swell of each of her hips as he drew her in. He wasn't watching her body move. Not now.

Instead, he looked into her eyes, and his *burned*, and she knew she was going to melt, utterly, and she wouldn't be able to do a thing to stop it. Not one thing, despite all her determination and her need to watch out for herself. And her memories, and the hurt, and all the things she couldn't trust herself to remember any more.

A smattering of applause indicated the end of the song. Zach lowered his hands. She realised hers were on his waist, let go and stepped back.

'You make shaking your hips an art form.' He smiled, making light of it, but his eyes didn't. They smouldered with dark feelings that showed her she hadn't seen past the first edge of this man. Not really, even though she had worked with him for three weeks and been aware of him for every moment of that time.

'Why don't you ask my brother to dance while I take Mum onto the floor? Dan's a bit shy about girls, but it would do him good to get out there with someone pretty and confident about herself.'

Zach's arms were locked to his sides, as though he didn't trust himself not to haul her back to him.

Confidence had been hard won in the last twelve months, but Lily thought: *you make me feel as though I am those things*, then turned and saw Daniel standing at the edge of the floor tugging at that collar again.

He was just a boy. Not yet in high school, probably. Without realising it revealed her own insecurity, she said, 'Will he let me that close, if I ask him?'

CHAPTER FIVE

'Yeah.' Zach answered Lily's question in a tone gravelled by the suppressed need inside him. 'I don't think Daniel will be able to do anything else.'

Lily didn't hear his words. She had already walked away, and that was probably just as well, because Zach really wasn't himself. He hadn't been himself since she'd walked into his office that first Monday and started to re-order his working life, as a matter of fact. And his comment hadn't been about Daniel, but about himself.

He had kissed Lily. Madly, deeply, in front of a room full of people. He wanted to do it again, in private, and never, ever stop. He couldn't convince himself to let it be. So he'd sent her away to dance with his brother, but so far separation didn't seem to be helping.

Lily headed straight for Daniel, hips wiggling, one arm stretched out to the boy as her finger beckoned him forward. It had the desired effect.

Daniel broke into a grin and was soon on the floor, laughing and showing her a few moves that weren't too bad for an eleven-year-old whose feet tended to get in his way. Zach closed his eyes on a familiar ache.

He was so proud of that kid.

With the need to whisk Lily out of the party and straight to the nearest available bed still thrumming deep in his veins, Zach tugged his mother onto the floor and tried to behave normally, instead of as though every nerve ending burned.

He had never wanted anyone this intensely. He would have taken anything Lily was willing to give him, if she had continued to look at him that way much longer after their shared kiss.

'Thanks, Mum.' He schooled his tone to sound nothing but cordial. 'This was nice of you.'

'I had a little help.' His mother let him twirl her out on the end of his arm, then pull her back in again, her laugh an echo that had lifted his spirits for as long as he could remember.

'Thank goodness Lily came along in time, because there's no way I could have asked that Rochelle creature.'

His mother didn't know about the sofa incident, but Zach could feel his ears burning anyway. 'Yeah, well, Rochelle's gone now, and I've got Lily instead. I hope she didn't have to do too much to help organise tonight.'

Again the protectiveness surged. He didn't want to add to Lily's worries, even though he was the one who had insisted she stay and work for him.

It's not the same thing.

His gaze moved automatically to Lily and Daniel, but it wasn't his brother he watched. It occurred to him that he might be truly out of his depth, but he pushed the idea away. This was a heady attraction, that was true, but it could be only that. He had learned his lesson with Lara.

'No, dear. I didn't make unreasonable demands on your Lily. All she needed to do was get you here.' The number ended and they made their way off the floor. 'Lily did seem a bit taken aback when I first outlined my plan. Does she have much family herself?'

'I don't know.' Suddenly it seemed wrong

that he didn't, yet why should it? 'She'll be gone soon. I really don't *need* to know.' But the words rang hollow, because he did want to know about her. He wanted it all. Her history, her secrets.

'I'm not sure if I know what I want,' he muttered, unaware he had spoken aloud.

'Well, my darling, I never thought you would go unscathed for ever. Now, remember we've got the barbecue tomorrow evening. That's still on, despite tonight's surprise. It'll be nice for the rellies who've travelled. Meanwhile, I think I'll start shooing people so we can all get some sleep before then.' And, with that curious mixture of remarks, his mother took herself off.

Zach moved off the dance floor slowly. He wanted Lily. That *was* all. Wasn't it?

Daniel brought Lily off the dance floor to join him, his elbow stuck out stiffly so she could grip it with her fingers. She did so with a soft smile on her face that caught at something deep inside Zach.

'Well done, Dan.' Zach's voice softened. 'I wish Dad could see you. He'd be really proud.'

'I wish he was here, too.' Daniel dropped his elbow, allowing Lily to step away, and his face tightened.

Zach kicked himself for reminding the kid of what he didn't have. He did his best to be father *and* brother to him, but he knew it was a poor second. 'Dan—'

'Did you read the brochure I left on the table at your place? The one about Sarrenden College? They've got the best mechatronics program in Australia, starting right from the first year of high school. The program's brand new.'

'I saw it, but it's in Melbourne, and we live here.' The building of all things mechanical and electronic was Daniel's latest obsession, and Zach was quite willing to indulge him, although Dan's interest would probably soon wane. 'We'll have to see if there's something here in Sydney. Maybe some after-school classes you could go to.'

Daniel's mouth tightened. He muttered, soft enough that only Zach heard, 'You don't understand.'

'Mechatronics is quite cutting-edge stuff, isn't it?' Lily addressed her question to Daniel. 'Wasn't one of last year's Youth Australia Innovation awards given to someone working in that field?'

Daniel's face lit up. 'Yeah. They designed this really cool computerised exercise "pet" that goes out with the person when they walk or jog. It has all-terrain capabilities, and it measures heart rate, blood pressure and a heap of other stuff. It "woofs" if anything is wrong with the person.'

'Speaking of exercise, do you want to take a run with me tomorrow morning?' Zach asked. 'I need to keep my fitness up for the match on Sunday.'

'Touch footy.' Daniel pulled a face. 'It's not *real* football. It's just a bunch of you and your suit friends running around pretending to be fit. Hockey's better.'

'Ah. The football jokes are explained.' At Daniel's side, Lily stifled a chuckle behind her hand. But the crinkling around her eyes revealed her amusement.

Since hockey was the only sport Daniel's senior class played at competitive level, Zach was reluctant to concede the point. 'Maybe, but in touch footy we still get to dive around in the mud if it's rained, and yell and swear a lot.'

A grin tugged at Daniel's mouth. 'I'll run with you,' he relented. 'But I'm not going to the game. And, right now, I'm going to find more food before they take it all away.'

'Off you go, then.' He gave Dan a friendly push towards the buffet table. 'There's still a bit of birthday cake left, I think.'

The hordes shooed rather well under his mother's efforts. Zach got caught up in a little flurry of goodbyes and good wishes. It was towards the end of this that he spotted Lily sidling away, and the feelings inside him roared in protest.

Not like this, just slipping away as though she meant nothing, as though the night and their shared kiss had meant nothing. As though either of them really believed this was over or in any way resolved. The buzz in his system assured him it was not.

His mother gathered Daniel and made her way to the elevator. Zach walked straight to Lily. He had her elbow in his hand before she noticed his presence. 'After a taxi? I'll get one.'

'Thank you, but there's no need to trouble yourself.' By the time she finished speaking, he had hustled her not towards the lift, where others waited to make a leisurely descent to the floor below, but to the ornate staircase. He didn't want to share her, even in this small way.

They descended without speaking. Her

heels clacked on the parquet steps. Their clothing rustled as they moved. It was oddly intimate, and his hand moved from her elbow and found its way to the small of her back as they stepped outside into the night.

The evening was warm with the promise of rain whispering on the sea breeze. After the rain, the temperature would drop, but for now the air caressed them, and drifted the scent of her perfume to him. Waves lapped against the wharf, adding to the feeling of intimacy.

Desire had him in its grip. He should leave her now, but he would see her home.

Among departing others, they were silent as they made their way to a row of cabs.

When they reached a vacant taxi, Lily gave a sigh that sounded rather relieved, and turned to him. 'Well, Happy Birthday again, and I guess I'll see you on Monday when things will be back to business as usual—although I do want to talk to you about the future in respect of that. I want to put Deborah—'

'We're not going there.' She wanted to cut and run? Not likely, and he might as well kill the idea now. Lily was a great secretary. He had no intention of losing her.

Besides, she was nervous. Aware. As awash

in all of this as he was. And he couldn't help but revel dangerously in that knowledge. He swept her before him into the rear seat of the cab and followed. 'Give the driver your address, there's a love.'

'Oh, but I—'

'Or we could go back to my place.' He wouldn't take her there. If he got her inside the doors of his home, he wasn't sure he could trust himself to let her go again. And, for all that he wanted her, that warning voice still had *some* volume remaining.

She must have taken his threat to heart, because she rattled off her address, a not particularly auspicious suburb near enough to the city centre to make commuting acceptable. What was her home like?

'You've not mentioned your family since you started working for me.' His mother's earlier question hovered in the back of his mind.

'There's not a lot to say.' Her tone held a curious flatness. 'I'm an only child. My parents don't live in Sydney. We keep in contact by phone, mostly. We're all busy with our own pursuits.'

Too busy to see each other in person at least sometimes? Was that by choice? If Lily were part of his family, he would want more than phone calls.

He might have questioned her more, but she looked at him then, and all he saw was the luminous quality of her eyes rendered almost indigo in the darkened interior of the cab. The need to kiss her rushed through him once again.

By the time the driver stopped outside a modest group of four old but large-looking flats in a quiet street, tension had filled the back of the cab.

Zach caught the driver's eye in the rear-view mirror. 'Keep the meter running. I won't be too long—'

'You don't need to be any time at all.' Lily's mouth was a mutinous line.

'A few minutes, perhaps.' Just long enough for a kiss goodnight. For a kiss without a room full of people to bring it to an end. A kiss that *he* ended, to prove that he could. To prove he had control over this. 'Which one's yours?'

'It's the first on the left, the one with the two external doors.'

'One for your home, and one for your office that can be accessed both from within and without?' He followed her up the short path, noted the splashes of brightly coloured flowers in beds on either side. He took her key from her and pushed it into the lock of the second door.

'Yes.' She gave a strained nod. 'That's right.'

A sticky note just below her lighted doorbell said 'catch the cat'. He read the words. Lily did, too, but they made little sense until he swung the door open and Lily bent, and with a deft movement snatched up a ball of tortoiseshell fluff as it tried to catapult itself past them.

'Jemima,' he said absently, and wanted to be held as closely. He wanted to be treasured by Lily, he realised, and shifted uneasily.

'If she got out, she might get run over. How do you know her name?' The question dropped with utter surprise from her mouth as she stepped inside and put the cat down.

He followed her in. 'You offered me Jemima's firstborn kitten if I'd give your agency another chance. You have a duck or a chicken, too, I think.'

'Oh. Oh, of course.' She swallowed. The cat wrapped around her ankles, then sat quietly on the floor beside her feet. 'Are you very fond of cats? I was going to get her spayed.'

She must be really rattled to be unable to remember their earlier conversation.

'You mentioned that.' His pulse quickened. 'In any case, I don't want a kitten.' What he wanted was Lily.

'I see.' She let out a breath, but her body remained tense, and her eyes…

She gave a nervous cough. 'Well, goodnight. Thank you for seeing me home.'

A glow of moonlight shone through the window behind her. He had seen nothing of her home besides the small bit of foyer they stood in and that extra door outside.

He wanted to see more, but most of all he wanted her. A growl erupted in his throat while his hands reached and pulled her forward. 'Lily. Tell me you want more than a taste of this. Tell me you've been thinking about it all night, too.'

Her skin was softer than he had even imagined. He discovered it inch by inch with the tips of his fingers. Touched the freckles he had fantasised about. A faint tremor followed the touch of his hands, a reaction that thrilled through him as well.

'I haven't wanted to think about it, but I have.' Her admission was reluctant but she remained before him, unable or unwilling to step away from his touch.

That small fact lodged inside him and took hold. He fingered the fabric of her gown where it clung lovingly below her neck. 'I like your dress. It reminds me of things the ladies used to wear to dinner when they came to our house when I was very small.'

Most of all, he liked the feel of the dress beneath his hands, and the thought of what she would feel like without it.

'The dress...the dress, ah...' Her words were breathless, strained with the same anticipation that had him in its grip. 'I, um, I won it on an eBay auction. UK, actually. I got Betty, my chicken, that way too. Not from the UK, from an online auction. Someone was going to *kill* her if I didn't buy her, and she lays the best eggs and is no trouble.'

She was full of surprises, full of adorable nervous talk, but right now there was only one thing about her that he wanted to know. One thing he wanted to unravel once and for all. 'I'm going to kiss you now, Lily. You might like to stop chattering while I do it.'

'Right.' The word was a sigh of defeat, or perhaps just acceptance as he pulled her close, and her hands rose to his chest to curl into the fabric of his formal jacket.

He wished the jacket away, and the dress shirt along with it. Zach wanted her touch on his skin, wanted it so much.

'Fall into it with me, Lily.' He lowered his head. 'If we must do this, let's do it together.'

'Together…' Lily was too fragile to risk being burned, and she suspected that could very easily happen, yet something inside her made her lift her face.

Warm lips closed over hers as though he had no choice about this, either. As though something deeper than conscious decision drove him.

His mouth was firm and delicious, and he gave it to her with an intimacy that wrapped dangerously around not only her senses, but her emotions. Her protests and concerns faded away in the face of his determined ministrations.

The kiss changed. His lips gentled against hers, and a wave of tenderness poured over her, through her. This shared intimacy reached right to the depths of her. Seemed more moving than any kiss she had shared, ever, and for a few wildly free moments she opened her heart to him.

She hadn't believed there could be more than their first kiss, but it had only been the prelude to this. To reconnecting to full, glorious life again in a way she hadn't done since a fateful kayaking trip twelve months ago.

A sigh slid through her lips, and her body relaxed into the firmness of his. Instead of fire he had given her a haven, and she wanted that so much.

And he kissed her. Oh, he kissed her so beautifully, as though he couldn't go another minute without having her lips pressed beneath his. As though he needed to have this, and couldn't live if it were denied him.

He kissed her as though she mattered, and she kissed him back. Yielded and demanded just as he did. She set aside everything. Her struggles, the fear that she could never be worthy.

She forgot that this feeling of rightness couldn't possibly be more than a fantasy, a chimera of her making. An illusion drawn from the desires of her heart, not from reality. But eventually that knowledge pushed its way forward, demanded to be heard.

This might feel real, but it wasn't. Because

she wasn't the whole person Zach thought her to be.

And he didn't want her in the way she longed to be wanted. Not with his heart and his soul and his feelings.

Hadn't he told her, that day at the pub, that he didn't want any kind of commitment with a woman? That he would never try that again? Lily remembered *that* quite clearly!

So what was she doing here, in his arms, laying herself emotionally bare while he couldn't possibly be engaged in the same way? If he knew her secrets, there was no way that he *could* want her like that.

Her eyes stung and she drew back, cursing her vulnerability and the ease with which she had chosen to ignore all that had shaped her life since she'd come to Sydney. 'I shouldn't have allowed this.'

Especially not here. This was her home. The one place she could be herself—if she shaved one leg twice, or thought she had washed her favourite pair of jeans and she hadn't, there was only her to know.

'You can't be here, Zach. I can't let you into this part of my life.' And if he started looking around, walked into the heart of her apartment and saw the reminder notices she'd posted up everywhere just so she could manage the most everyday of things—check for eggs after breakfast, wash clothes on Saturdays, buy groceries Sundays—he would see that it was no ordinary life. 'Please, will you—?'

'Stop? Leave?' He stepped back, his chest rising and falling with each sharp breath. He ran one slightly unsteady hand through his hair. Shadows filled his eyes, sharpened his features. 'God knows I don't want to, Lily.'

She searched his face for reasons for that reluctance. The sting of desire coloured his cheeks, formed his features in tightness, particularly around his mouth and nose. His mouth looked both softer, and tougher, than before. And in his eyes…

Banked heat. Shadows. She didn't know what they meant, but, even as she looked, his body tensed and a hooded expression came over his face.

'You want physical satisfaction.' She schooled her voice to sound simply as though she were stating a fact. She wanted fulfilment with him, too, but she wasn't wired for only that.

'This is just an attraction thing, a physical

thing. If it was more…' She trailed off, and, yes, some small, hidden portion of her soul wanted him to say she was wrong. That he *did* have feelings for her and wanted to pursue those feelings, and that was what this had been all about.

He didn't. He just watched her silently, every muscle clenched, that harshness of their first day's meeting back on his face. He balled both fists at his sides, took a step towards her. Then he seemed to fight with himself for a moment before he stepped back again.

A small, silent cry reverberated inside her because of that rejection, even though she had expected nothing else. 'I think you'd better go.'

He hesitated, half-turned, one hand gripping the door frame. But eventually, just as she had known he would, he went.

Lily busied herself with the nightly routine of settling her animals, ensuring all was locked up securely, and with her notebook by the bed before she climbed in.

If she lay awake staring at the ceiling most of the night, well, that was her concern, and the time wasn't wasted. She used it to remind herself of the importance of getting out of

Zach's orbit. Not just because of what had happened tonight, but for the sake of her agency as well.

First thing Monday morning, she would tell Zach he had to accept Deborah in her place at the office. Surely, given what had happened tonight, and given that she had got things in order in his office for him, Zach would agree?

Then Lily would put any lingering feelings for him behind her and get on with her life. And the damaged state of her brain and memory would remain her painful secret.

CHAPTER SIX

'I need to talk to you. I've been thinking all weekend, and I've decided—'

'I'm glad you're here early, because we've got a hell of a day—' Zach broke off.

Shoulders tensed and thrown back, Lily strode to stand directly before his desk, her chin hitched high. She wore a simple navy dress in some sort of knit fabric. Was she aware that by its plain severity it made him want to see what lay beneath? He schooled his features to reveal nothing of his thoughts.

'When we first discussed replacing Rochelle, I mentioned bringing Deborah Martyn in here. I know you weren't initially keen on the idea, but now that I've straightened out the office and have things running efficiently...' She smoothed her hands down the sides of her dress. Tension bracketed the mouth that had melted under his on Friday night.

'You want me to take Deborah in your place.' He almost kept the growl from his tone, but couldn't stop himself from rising from his chair. A moment later, he leaned against the edge of the desk near to where she stood.

Close. Casual. Yet his body thrummed in recognition of hers. A silent warning reverberated through him as he faced her: *She wanted him to leave?* 'It's not going to happen, Lily.'

He reached out to toy with the small dictation recorder resting on his desk. Flipped the cassette lid open, closed it again and finally tossed the article aside. 'We've covered this ground.'

'I know, but that was at the beginning. There's no reason she shouldn't step into the role now.' Wariness haunted her gaze, tightened the muscles of her face and neck. 'I've discussed it with Deb, and she's able to replace me as soon as I give her the word. You won't suffer any lag time. Indeed, I'll stay here for an hour or so once Deb arrives. Show her the ropes. Let her know how everything works.'

'You'll give me a nice clean-cut change over, in fact.' He came to his feet. Made no concession to how close together that put them. Said in tones of gravel and sandpaper, because this was what it was all about and they both knew it, 'If you want me to apologise for kissing you—'

'It's got nothing to do with that.' She tipped her head back but otherwise held her ground.

Her strength fired through him, made him want her all the more. The defiance and denial fooled neither of them, but he admired it.

'I think it does.' His weekend had been haunted by memories of holding her, kissing her. Zach needed to get those memories under control, bring what had happened back into a sense of reality, instead of viewing it as utterly mind-blowing.

He turned his head to look out the windows. The washed-out horizon met his gaze. No, he wouldn't let her go. It wasn't that he *couldn't*. He wasn't willing to accept the disruption to his work place. There was nothing emotional in either his decision, or the way he had reacted when he'd kissed her. He was too smart to let there be. Wasn't he?

When he turned back to her, his face was schooled to show only rejection of her desire to leave. 'We had an agreement, Lily. You must know I won't let you break it. Don't you think the weeks you've spent learning your way around the office count for anything?

'A new person, no matter how good or how skilled, would still need to orient themselves. I'm not prepared to lose valuable time to that. You agreed to my terms.' He reminded her of it quietly. 'If you break them, I *will* consider you in breach of contract with my company.'

'You kissed me.' Her accusation came on a ragged whisper. 'You broke your own rules.'

'We kissed each other. It was mutual. If it happens again, it will also be mutual.' He stared down his nose at her and tried not to think of her freckles, of the taste of her and the softness of her skin beneath his hands. 'And you just said it wasn't about that.'

'No, I didn't. I—' She broke off and looked uneasy, then waved one hand in dismissal. 'What I said isn't the point. It would be wiser for me to go.' Her frustration showed in the low, impatient sound she made… 'But, as you clearly don't share that opinion, and you know you have me locked in, let me just say this.' Her eyes narrowed into warning slits. 'There will be no repeat performance of that kiss between us.'

She turned. Her body quivered with whatever feelings she fought to suppress and, oh, Zach wanted to unleash it all. To let it free and lose himself in her. Maybe he did have feelings…

But he couldn't let himself do that. He didn't acknowledge her statement directly. Instead, he turned away too. 'Now that this conversation's over, perhaps we can get some work done.'

For the rest of the morning, they worked hard and spoke only when necessary. Zach buried himself in paperwork and told himself he didn't have to want her. That his growing admiration for her didn't have to mean he was becoming emotionally involved, either.

When, ever, had it been other than choice for him to want any woman? There was no reason Lily should be any different. If she truly wasn't interested, he didn't have to be, either.

Just before lunch time, the phone rang. Zach happened to glance at Lily as she answered it. He wasn't addicted to the sight of her, nor had he stolen countless other glances since the start of the day. A man needed to keep an eye on his business, including what his secretary was doing with her time. That was all.

'Mark.'

She put such warmth into the name that the hair on the back of Zach's neck stood up. There was a short pause as she listened to the voice on the other end of the line.

Then a smile like sunshine crossed her expressive face. 'Oh, I'd love to. Now? That would be wonderful. I'll see you soon.'

Zach turned his back on her. He snatched up a file and carried it to his windows, although he did no more than flip it open and pretend to give the first page his attention.

When an older man walked into the office minutes later, Lily flew out of her chair and straight into the man's arms. In response, he pecked Lily's cheek in an avuncular manner, and stepped back to smile at her.

Their obvious close friendship brought a surge of unexpected jealousy to Zach. He tossed down the folder and joined them before he could examine that reaction. 'Hello. I'm Zachary Swift, Lily's boss.'

'Mark Uden. It's a pleasure to meet one of Lily's assignments.' The man shook hands and withdrew.

Zach found he didn't like being referred to as an 'assignment.' He didn't like the man's salt-and-pepper hair and air of mature sophistication, either, which was quite irrational of him.

Lily collected her bag from her desk and hurried to Uden's side. 'We should get going.'

Before Zach could do anything, she muttered a farewell in his general direction and swept out of the office, her arm entwined with Uden's.

Zach returned to his desk and ploughed his way through a stack of work, and a cheese and salad focaccia delivered from the building's twentieth-floor cafeteria. He swilled down orange juice and glared at the city stretched beyond his windows, his mood out of sorts for no good reason.

So Lily had flown to Uden as though the man were some sort of sanctuary. So what? Surely Zach didn't want to be the one she ran to, because that really would suggest a desire for emotional closeness, and he wasn't in a position to go there.

Who was Uden, anyway? What place did he have in Lily's life? Zach wanted to know, but he had no hold over Lily. She didn't owe it to him to tell him about her friends. Telling himself to put Lily and everything to do with her out of his mind, Zach lobbed the crushed juice bottle into his waste-paper basket.

Just before Lily was due back from her break, Zach's phone rang. When he ended the call, he got up to prowl his office again.

Lily's soft footfalls as she returned to the office brought his pacing to an abrupt halt. He stepped into her office, and stopped just short of her desk. 'You omitted to give me a telephone message about a meeting scheduled for this afternoon straight after lunch.'

She gave a startled gasp, and swung to face him. The large, soft handbag she had been about to slip into the desk drawer dropped from her fingers and hit the carpet. 'Perhaps there's some misunderstanding? I don't remember anything about a meeting.'

As she spoke, she snatched up the phone message pad and began to search it frantically.

'You won't find anything there.' Zach drew closer, aware he was being unreasonable, but unable to stop himself. He *was* jealous of Uden, of the time Lily had spent in the older man's company, and he didn't much like himself for it. 'I've already checked.'

'I apologise for the oversight.' A haunted expression filled her eyes. 'If you'll tell me what needs to be done in preparation, I'll do my best to be organised in time for the meeting. And if you want to mark this against my record, against my company's record, I understand.'

The depth of Lily's remorse made him face where his jealousy had taken him. What was one small slip-up in the scheme of things? He wasn't angry at her over some stupid phone message about a meeting he already knew about, and had no need to prepare for. He hated the idea that she might trust and confide in anyone but him. His attitude shamed him.

'Lily.' He looked into her eyes. Saw the shadowed hurt reflected there, and knew he had caused it. His hands lifted towards her.

But a clerk hustled into the room, begging Lily's assistance with some information on one of their most urgent projects. She retrieved a large file from her desk, and they bent their heads over it.

Zach looked at his watch. The chance to apologise was lost; he needed to leave for his meeting. On a rare bout of uncertainty, the issue unresolved and sitting uncomfortably in his gut, he murmured a farewell and left.

* * *

An hour later, Zach's finance manager continued to drone on. Zach struggled to focus on the words, but all he could think about was Lily. He felt like a particularly ugly, beastly dog that had attacked a kitten for no good reason.

In the middle of the other man's speech about profit and loss, Zach tossed down the remaining sheets of paper and got to his feet. 'Just do whatever you feel is necessary with the rest, Steele. I have to go.'

He made his way back to his suite of offices in record time. 'Lily—'

'I'm glad you're back. I've just received a call from Gunterson and Greig.' She had a phone message clasped in her hand, an urgent expression on her face, and she kept the width of her desk between them.

She scanned the message before she continued. 'They say they're awaiting a formal expression of interest from you in relation to their Mulligan project, and will seek another buyer if they don't have your offer to table at their board meeting first thing tomorrow morning. I don't remember anything at all about this project.'

'The report was supposed to go out the week Rochelle was here.' Clearly it hadn't, and somehow Zach had overlooked following up on it as well. He had compiled the facts and figures and dictated the report. But it had never turned up typed on his desk.

This lapse of his was a much worse infraction than Lily forgetting that small, not particularly significant, phone message.

Lily seemed to sag with relief. 'I'll check for a paper file. If I can't find one, there may be something on computer.' She moved towards the filing cabinet. 'It's no use going through audio tapes, unless you've got any tucked away in your office that might still have a recording on them from weeks ago.'

Her lovely, straight back was presented to him as she began to riffle through the contents of the top drawer of the first filing cabinet.

Zach clenched his fists against the desire to reach for her. To run his fingers down the length of her spine, to cup her shoulders and turn her into his arms.

He had wanted a physical closeness with Lily from the day they'd met. Now he admitted he *did* want other things from her and with her. Things he couldn't have in his wildest dreams, yet somewhere deep inside he *did* dream of them. Lily was quirky and special, dedicated, intense. And somehow, over all of that, she was hugely vulnerable. He didn't know why, but he saw glimpses of that vulnerability when her guard was down.

All these things attracted him, but Zach couldn't get involved in her life. Even so, he had to apologise. He directed low-spoken words at that very straight back. 'I acted like an ass, Lily, going off about one stupid message. I was out of line, and I hope you'll forgive me.'

She turned. Vulnerability shadowed her eyes. For long moments, she searched his face and seemed somehow torn. Finally, she nodded. 'Apology accepted. Now, we need to work out what to do about this Mulligan problem.' Her fingers continued their busy search of the files in the cabinet.

Zach watched those fingers move, and wanted them on his skin instead. He couldn't resist reaching for her, even though he knew it was dangerous to touch her when he didn't have his desire under control.

He touched her arm, gently turned her to face him. Said her name again. He wanted to ask her about Uden. Wanted to tell her again how sorry he was. Most of all, he just wanted to hold her close. 'Lily, my dear.'

'Please, Zach. Don't.' She turned tortured eyes to his face. 'If you hold me, I'll be lost, and I—I'm not for you. Besides, you made it clear you don't want to get involved, even if I don't really understand why.'

'After my relationship with Lara fell apart I made up my mind I wouldn't put myself or another woman in that position again.' Zach didn't know if explaining it would help or just make things harder. 'I'm a career man, with the responsibility of a widowed mother and a young brother to contend with. Those things fill my life and always will. Unfortunately, knowing that doesn't seem to be making any difference to the fact that I desire you.'

'I see. And, for me, just wanting someone is nowhere near enough. I guess that makes it pretty clear we have no common meeting ground with each other.' She turned away again, searched through the cabinet almost desperately, her agitation revealed in the swiftly moving fingers. In the death grip she had on the edge of the cabinet with her other hand.

Finally, her fingers stopped moving. She

stared at him while he fought with himself, fought his need. And she seemed to be fighting hers.

'Hello.' His mother entered the room, breaking the taut silence. 'I'm glad I've found you together.'

A newspaper clutched in her hand, she glanced from his face to Lily's tense frame. 'Have I interrupted?'

It was Lily who stepped forward, and forced a smile to her face. 'Hello, Anne. How lovely to see you again. You haven't interrupted. You've found us with a work problem to sort out, that's all.'

As she spoke, she retreated behind her desk and sank into the chair. She tugged her notebook forward and held it tightly. 'We've just discovered a deadline that needs to be met, and there's not much time.'

'Oh.' Anne looked at Zach with a hint of puzzlement. 'You won't be able to come to the school, then, to watch the hockey match.'

CHAPTER SEVEN

'DAMN. I don't know how I can be there, and take care of this problem too.' Zach *never* ignored a commitment to his brother. He had never forgotten one before, either, but this had slipped his mind as all his attention centred on Lily. His computer diary would have beeped him a reminder, but even so…

'Well, I'll just explain, dear. Daniel will understand.' His mother forced a bright smile, and pushed the paper into his hands. 'I must be off so I don't miss the start of the game myself, but you'll want to see this. There's a lovely little article about your birthday in the society column on page eight, with some photos.'

Zach took the paper automatically and spoke quickly, before his mother could get out the door. 'Tell Daniel I'll be there.' He would figure out a way. His computer beeped that reminder as he spoke.

His mother left. Zach stuffed the Mulligan notes into his briefcase and cleared his desk, locking away anything that shouldn't be left for the nightly visit of the cleaners.

He could feel Lily's gaze on him, and glanced up. 'I can't believe my own stupidity. It makes me twice as angry at myself for the way I spoke to you earlier. About the phone message, and about—'

'It doesn't matter.' She cut him off quickly. 'Maybe it's a good thing that we cleared the air. We really do need to accept that there's no way forward for these…reactions we have to each other, and put them behind us. But, Zach, when did you say that offer has to be tabled?'

'First thing tomorrow.' He could put something together this evening, but it would take hours for him to type it into his computer, and it would still need to be tidied into a professional looking document before morning. 'Lily, it's not that easy to ignore a hunger that has both of us on edge the whole time we're together.'

'Yes, it is. It has to be.' But her eyes were wild and filled with the very hunger she so adamantly wanted to deny. She took a deep

breath. 'Now, I'll come along to the school. I
have a small computer note pad in my bag,
although I don't use it often. You can dictate
the offer while you watch the game. I can type
it straight in. Then all I'll need to do is come
in early tomorrow, upload it to the computer
and format it properly, then print it out. You
can sign it, and it can go by courier and be
there when they open for the day.'

It was a good solution. It was the only one
he could see would work, and he would be a
fool to reject it. But did she really believe they
could switch off what they felt for each other?
Zach could disprove that theory in about three
seconds flat. For now, he stuck to business, as
Lily seemed determined to do. 'I don't like to
ask you to put yourself out that way.'

She finished making a note in her diary,
quickly tidied her desk, and turned to face him.
The heat in her eyes remained, but she had
done her best to bank it. 'You didn't. I volunteered.'

During the drive in his car, Lily, notebook
in one hand, phone in the other, worked her
way through a number of text messages on her
cell phone. He heard her mutter things like,
'Good work, Deb,' and, 'Good to know every-

thing's going well,' as she made the occasional note. And Zach realised that he relished simply being near her, whatever she happened to be doing.

He parked the car near the school and got out, his gaze searching the grounds for his mother. Lily returned her cell phone and notebook to her bag and joined him.

'I appreciate this, Lily.' He took a step towards her.

'It's no trouble.' She cast one trembling glance in his direction, then hurried onto the school grounds and made a beeline for the huddle of parents already congregated in the observation stands at the edge of the oval.

The appreciation in Zach's tone touched a chord deep inside Lily. She needed to feel valued, and, despite being sharp with her earlier, Zach had made it clear he did appreciate her. He just apparently believed there was no escaping their attraction to each other, which was something that made Lily rather uneasy. 'Let's greet your mother and find some seats.'

Once they were seated on the painted wooden-slat benches that stretched across the sheltered stands, Lily decided she had better check her phone messages. She drew the phone out and caught Zach giving her an odd look.

There were no messages, and she quickly realised she must have already checked through them. Well, she would have written anything down if needed. 'I was just checking the time.'

'Looks like the game is about to start.' Zach drew her attention to the teams on the field. 'There's Daniel.' The pride in his voice was completely unconscious, and made something deep inside her tighten with longing. He clearly loved his family.

The two teams moved onto the field. Daniel looked up and seemed to immediately find his brother, and his mother, seated some rows away.

Lily forced her lips to smile. 'Is Daniel a good hockey player?'

'He's good enough.' Zach's grin suggested he thought his brother was a great player.

'Maybe we should look at the article your mother gave you.' Lily reached for the paper, and flicked through it until she found the article.

'Yes. Let's have a look.' Zach lowered his head to examine the article and photos.

Lily's interest in the article warred with

more immediate ones. The knowledge of that head bent close to hers tingled through her. She could feel the heat of his body, could smell not only the scent of his cologne but also the pine-scented shampoo he used on his hair, and the fresh, clean scent of his skin that was uniquely Zach.

Her stomach pitched with a feeling of sharp awareness. His arm bumped hers as he moved closer to study the paper.

It wasn't easy to focus on the article when all she wanted to do was turn and look into Zach's eyes, and see if they reflected the awareness she felt. So much for fighting her reactions to him! 'It's a nice wrap-up of the party.'

One photo showed a group of people at the buffet. Another had her and Daniel grooving down, big grins on their faces. The last was of Zach and his mother, dancing beyond her and Daniel.

Lily doubted that a casual observer would have even guessed that the intent look on Zach's face had been directed right at her. She hadn't been aware of it herself, at the time. Or, rather, she hadn't been aware of that specifically. It had been more of an overall sense of unbreakable connection to him.

'I'm looking at you as though I want to swallow you whole.' As Zach moved to look more closely, his leg pressed against hers from thigh to knee. 'When it comes to you, I can't seem to control that hunger. I've tried.'

'W-well.' What could she say to such an honest statement? Particularly when it made her entire body sing with recognition. When she refused to look at him, Zach's fingers closed around the delicate bones of her wrist, clasping while he waited for her response.

It could have been intended as a comforting gesture. Lily's sensory reaction made it impossible for her to tell. All she could feel was his gaze on her, his body against her. His touch on that super-soft skin at the inner side of her wrist.

With effort, she raised her gaze to his. 'Look. The game has started. You'd best watch, or your brother will be disappointed.'

With a frustrated murmur, Zach turned his attention to the field.

Lily watched the game too, and lost herself for a little while in the fierce efforts of the boys on both teams.

'Daniel's very determined. Look at the way he goes after the ball.' She watched the boy jump nimbly into the air and whack the ball away from an opponent, and felt Zach's pride as they both clapped.

Play moved to the far end of the field again.

Zach glanced at the electronic note pad on her lap. 'Let's get this offer down.'

He dictated between play and, scared she might lose it all and not be able to remember any of it, Lily saved her work frequently.

Eventually the work was saved for the final time, the mini-computer tucked safely away in her bag.

'Thanks for your help.' He glanced at her briefly before turning his attention back to the game.

It got cold. Zach removed his suit coat and wrapped it around her shoulders, and she sank into the scent and warmth of him, and wondered what was happening to her.

She and Richard had enjoyed the typical intimacies to be expected of any committed couple, sporadically, and there hadn't been skyrockets. But surely that was the stuff of fantasies, anyway? So why did the simplest touch from Zach, or just the scent of him, affect her so strongly?

As the match progressed to tied scores,

tension in the stands escalated. Lily's tension climbed too, but for a different reason.

When Daniel scored the winning goal with just seconds of play remaining, Zach gave a hoarse roar, and Lily's own shout startled her.

She told herself it was the pleasure of the moment that had them in each other's arms, laughing. But a moment later that embrace changed completely, and Zach let out a feral growl as he drew almost roughly away from her. 'Do you see now, Lily, that this can't be simply shut off? I think we'd better be on our way, now.'

He didn't give her time to think. Just made for his brother and congratulated him. 'Well done, Dan.'

'Thanks.' The boy's pride was subdued. 'It's good exercise. I suppose I don't mind it.'

'Your brother seems a little melancholy?' Lily brought it up during the drive to her house, but Zach shrugged the question off.

'Dan's just growing up. He was probably embarrassed about his win today. Boys get like that.' He stopped the car. 'You've gone above and beyond the call of duty today. I'll be here to collect you tomorrow at seven-thirty, so we have time to organise the report and get it couriered.'

'I can catch an early train.' Her bag banged against her hip when she got out of the car, and she thought of Zach's firm thigh pressed against her.

His mouth tightened. 'You could, but I'd rather make it easy for you to get to work without any difficulties.' He paused. 'You don't drive, do you?'

'Oh, I can drive. It's just that I sold—' She straightened and turned away, shocked that she had almost told him about selling her car to finance the start of her business.

He climbed out of the car after her, caught her wrist in the circle of his fingers. Her pulse beat rapidly. Could he feel it?

'What if we explored the attraction, Lily? It might be a good way to get it out of both our systems.' His fingers stroked her soft flesh.

'Do you think that would help?' Each time he touched her, she wanted him more. She suspected a conscious exploration of their interest would only escalate it.

His gaze held hers. 'All I can think about is this.'

He didn't rush her. His hands invited her forward, but it was her choice to move close to him. When the heat in his eyes and the tight awareness on his face made it clear he wanted to kiss her, she was the one who lifted up, who pressed her lips against his in that first, reckless acceptance.

'I think this is the only feeling that's been right in my world since I met you.' The harsh admission was whispered against her cheek before he lowered his head again.

'Zach.' Even though she knew it was fool-hardy, Lily gave in to the instinct that encouraged her closer.

He tightened his hold, drew her up against him, so that every part of her was pressed close. She welcomed it all. Their kiss changed, mouths softened. She gave vent to a tiny whimper of need.

'I could look into your eyes and drown in you and never stop.' His admission shook a tremor from her. 'I've never wanted to make love with a woman so much. I want to take you to my bed.'

'No. No… I don't want…that from you.' It was too intimate for the kind of temporal involvement Zach would want. Her body might say yes, but she had to listen to the warning of her mind. Her defences belatedly kicked in again. She backed away from him.

But Zach had only stated the truth. That he wanted her. And it wasn't that statement of truth that scared her. It was her temptation, despite everything, to yield to him and take whatever he was willing to give.

CHAPTER EIGHT

ZACH dropped a tape and several Manila folders into the tray on Lily's desk. Lily was delivering documents to Steele on the finance floor. She'd been gone about five minutes, and already Zach missed seeing her here at her desk.

He had it bad. With a sigh, he picked up the sticky note pad on her blotter, jotted the time and date and stuck it to the tape, then grinned a little at himself. Sometimes it was a case of Lily training him to do things *her* way.

Without stopping to think about it, he dropped into her chair and did a full three-hundred-and-sixty-degree slow swivel on it. The scent of lily of the valley clung to the fabric back of the chair. Zach closed his eyes and inhaled.

In the days since his brother's school hockey

competition, he had tried to leave her alone, to forget her. But he still desired her. Still noticed her every move, still tracked her through the days whether he chose to or not, and dreamed of her through the long nights.

Maybe he should capitulate about having one of her other workers in to replace her. Yet, even as he thought it, he knew he wasn't ready to let her out of his life.

'Hello. Is Lily not here at the moment?' The familiar voice sounded from in front of the desk.

Zach snapped his eyes open and stared into Mark Uden's calm face. 'Ah, Uden. Good afternoon. No. She's delivering something on another floor, then we'll be packing up for the day.'

'I thought I'd give Lily a lift to her volunteer session at the institute.' Uden paused, and added, 'I saw your photographs in the paper the other day. Let's see, page eight, the society column, wasn't it? Many happy returns for your birthday. I hope it was an enjoyable event.'

'It was. Thanks.' Zach rose from the chair, but remained standing behind the desk. 'You appear to have a good memory.' And what did Uden mean about a volunteer session? What institute?

'I have a natural gift for all types of recall. Faces, places, names, dates. I've never used a diary in my life.' Uden gave a self-effacing smile. 'I confess, some of my colleagues find my ability quite aggravating at times. I try to keep the knowledge of that skill from my patients, of course. No need to make them uncomfortable.'

'Lily wouldn't last long if she tried that, but she does a great job with her diaries and calendars and sticky notes.' Zach *liked* her zany, intense commitment to recording just about everything that happened in her day.

It wasn't that odd. He scowled, recalling her commitment to her work, and his fixation on everything *but* her work, his fixation on Lily.

'She's confided in you!' Uden's smile was blinding. 'I'm so pleased to know that. Lily is usually very secretive about her history, you know.'

Lily's history? What could Uden be implying about Lily? Did the man mean her past engagement?

'Lily told me about her past, yes.' He refused to pretend that he found any pleasure in the knowledge that Lily had cared for someone once and maybe still did. He raised an eyebrow.

'Whether she's over it or not is open to question.'

Uden rocked back on the heels of his shoes. 'It's not really a case of getting over it. Rather, it's about making adjustments. Because of the injury to her brain, she's had to completely rebuild her confidence. That will take a long time, a lot longer than the year that has passed so far since her accident.'

'What?' Zach's gaze narrowed. They were clearly at cross purposes. What was Uden talking about? 'What do you mean, an injury? An accident?'

'Ah, I beg your pardon.' Uden drew himself up. 'Did you not just state that Lily had confided in you?'

'Lily told me about her *ex-fiancé*. I thought that was the history you meant, when you suggested she had confided in me. She hasn't said a word about anything else.' Zach faced the older man, stunned, unable to absorb that one, shocking truth. Lily injured. Her brain damaged.

It couldn't be true. He knew her. Had worked with her, seen her skills, her ability. Yet, even as Zach thought this, he recalled so many incidents that had meant nothing at the time.

Lily having to leave a note on her door to make sure she didn't let her cat get run over. Her difficulty remembering barrages of names or instructions. The way she had tried to check her phone messages twice before Dan's hockey game.

Zach felt awe and deep heartache for all Lily must have endured. He wanted to hold her close and protect her from ever being harmed again. He wanted to tell her she was incredible. But if Lily ever knew that he had accidentally uncovered her secret…

'I must ask you not to speak of what you've just learned to anyone, especially not to Lily.' Uden's face had paled. 'I might wish she would trust people more easily with the truth of her condition, but this still should have been her story to tell, if and when she was ready.'

'It's not your fault. I won't say anything to her, there's no reason she need ever know.' But Zach wanted to ask Lily about it, to understand, to offer support and comfort and encouragement…

'Mark! What's going on? Why are you swearing Zach to secrecy? What have you told him about me?' Lily's strident words brought Zach's head around in abrupt attention.

She barely looked at him. Instead, her glance slewed to the man at Zach's side. 'Mark?'

Lily could have heard everything. Zach had been too absorbed in Uden's shocking revelation to notice anything around them. All he knew was the hurt on her face now, and the need to make this situation right. 'Lily.'

'My dear…' Mark's voice trembled through pinched lips.

She looked at the older man with betrayal in her eyes. 'You did tell him! How could you?'

Uden's expression confirmed it. 'It wasn't intentional, my dear. I called in to ask if you'd like to ride with me to the institute and grab a bite at our cafeteria before you do your volunteer session. Your employer and I misunderstood each other, and I'm afraid I told him something I shouldn't have.'

Lily held a large envelope in her hands. She lowered it to the desk with excessive care, and turned to face Zach as though she thought she might fly apart at any second. Accusation made her words sharp. 'How dare you mislead Mark into blurting information about me?'

Her voice trembled at the end. Unshed tears pooled in eyes that seemed to have lost all their vivacity and had filled, instead, with deep hurt. 'You had no right to pry into my affairs, and now you'll *know*.'

She came to a choked stop.

Zach took an automatic step towards her. He wanted to comfort her, to make this right, but she was so upset. 'It was a mistake. I thought—' He reached out a hand, but sensed her withdrawal even before she stepped back to avoid his touch.

'You thought what—that you would find out just who Mark was and what he had to do with me? All because I went to lunch with him?'

Zach *had* been jealous of a relationship he now realised must have started as that of mentor and student, and progressed to friendship. Lily must have studied under Mark Uden in order to learn to function again after her accident. What exactly had happened?

Zach didn't try to defend himself. This wasn't about that, anyway. 'I meant you no harm, Lily. I can only repeat that, and hope you believe me.'

Uden cleared his throat, and Lily turned her head towards him. 'It's all right, Mark. Why don't you go? I'll be there for my session, but I don't feel like eating first.'

The older man hesitated, then after a moment nodded and left the office.

But it wasn't all right. Zach waited until Uden's footsteps receded before he spoke again. 'Lily, please believe I would never have pried deliberately, and I'm sure your mentor wouldn't have betrayed you, either. It was a very short conversation, stopped the moment we both realised what had happened.'

'The end result is the same, isn't it? You know my brain doesn't work like it should. That I'm flawed and always will be.' She drew in deep gulps of air. Harsh spots of colour dotted each cheek, alabaster whiteness behind them.

'I'd like to understand about your injury.' *So I can help you. So I don't blunder around and hurt you, as I must have done the day I got angry at you for forgetting to write down a stupid phone message.*

'I'm so sorry, Lily.' A great well of protectiveness rose up, and Zach realised that he did care about her. That he cared *for* her. Wanted her in ways he had never wanted another woman. It wasn't love. It couldn't be that. But it was something outside of his experience, it was strong, and he wondered if he could control it.

He should exorcise those feelings now, but how could he, when he only wanted to take her pain away?

Silently, Lily moved past him and retrieved her bag from the drawer of her desk. Anger, pride and a great woundedness surrounded her as she shut down her computer. 'I don't want to talk about this any more. I can't think about it. I—I have to go.'

Zach wanted to find some way to get through to her and ease her hurt. But her hands around the straps of her handbag were clenched to whiteness, her expression haunted, and he knew now wasn't the time. He stood back and let her leave.

'Naturally, now that you know my situation, you'll feel it's best if I remove myself from your office immediately.' Lily had thought long and hard about how to handle this interview with Zach. She had lain awake much of the night, plotting and planning, and crying into her pillow, while Jemima batted at her head with a kindly paw, as though to say, *what's wrong? How can I help?*

Dawn had found Lily dry-eyed and determined. She had phoned Zach at his home. Had asked him to meet her at a coffee shop near his work at eight a.m., and had disconnected before he could ask questions.

Now they sat here, their knees almost touching beneath the small square table. Men and women in business clothing bustled in, bustled out, coffee in paper cups clutched in their hands as they anticipated the first caffeine fix of the day.

Few sat, and she and Zach had found a table tucked into a corner away from the general bustle. The coffee shop was redolent with the scents of ground coffee-beans, vanilla, and sweet pastries. Lily nursed her mocha caramel latte and knew she shouldn't have chosen it.

The warm, sweet smells inside the shop might promise enticing, creamy delights, but her rebellious stomach had other ideas and was twisted quite firmly into resistant knots. Lily would have been hard pressed to choke down a regular coffee at the moment, let alone this sweet, cream-topped version.

'That's why you wanted to meet early here this morning? To say you want to leave?' Zach pushed aside his sensible, simple cappuccino and examined her with a deep, penetrating gaze that seemed to want to see right into the very heart of her.

It wasn't fair that over the top of all the other, stronger scents she could detect his aftershave lotion. *That* made her stomach tighten in quite a different way.

'Why?' He went on. 'Just because I know there's a reason you write yourself a few sticky notes to ensure you stay on track?'

'It's a lot more than a few reminder notes!' Oh, she had been right to want to replace herself. If he had agreed then, she would have been gone before he'd known anything about her past. Already she could see a difference in the way he looked at her.

Zach leaned forward. His gaze seemed to contain a great deal of understanding—the pitying kind!

'I won't pretend that what I learned yesterday doesn't change things.' The softened tone of his voice confirmed her fears. He did pity her.

When he spoke, it only made it worse. 'I'll treat you differently from now on.'

'You don't feel the same way about me.' How *could* he still want her, now that he knew of her condition? 'I understand, Zach. You don't have to explain.'

'Thank you. It's hard to articulate…' He watched her silently for a moment, before relief slowly bloomed across his face. 'You have my respect, Lily. I think you're amazing, coping the way you do. This is very mature of you. I just…I don't want either of us to feel uncomfortable.'

This was just what every girl didn't want to hear. Next thing, Zach would say he hoped they would stay friends. She decided to head that one off before it happened. 'I'm glad we had this conversation. It's always good to take the chance to clear the air.'

Zach seemed to hesitate, and said quietly, 'Before we talk about work any further, would you explain your situation to me? I'd like to know exactly how extensive your…difficulties are.'

'But I'll be leaving. Surely you don't need to know all that?' Panic welled inside her at the thought of exposing the details of her condition.

'You'll be staying to the end of the agreed time.' Zach sounded very calm as he tossed this statement down. 'But, as your employer, I think I should know how your condition affects you.'

'And how it might impact on my work for you.' An angry, determined part of Lily rose up and pointed out that she could do very close to as good a job as anybody else, even if she did go about things differently. 'I volunteered to leave. That's why I asked for this meeting. To let you know Deborah could take over now.'

'You may have decided that.' His voice softened to a silken thread. 'But I don't recall being consulted, and, as it happens, I don't consider it to be in my best interests to have to undergo a further change in staffing right at the moment.'

'Why not? Deborah—'

'I'll explain my reasons.' His gaze again pierced her. 'After you outline your condition to me.'

'Fine. I'll explain.' She didn't see what difference it would make, and Zach clearly did have a changed view of her now. Maybe he was able to simply forget he had ever desired her, and was willing to put up with her idiosyncrasies to avoid that further change of staff he had mentioned?

She kept her chin up, and hoped he couldn't see how much all this was hurting her. 'I have damage to a large portion of the short-term memory area of my brain. The majority of things that would normally be retained there now get forgotten instead.'

Zach gave a tight nod. 'Go on.'

Lily drew a deep breath. 'I've learned some patterns of things I'll regularly forget, and worked out ways to counteract the problem with those things. I leave a "memory trail". A notebook beside my bed at night. Other reminders are posted all over my apartment, and I employ the same style of reminders at work.'

Lily hated having to talk about this, and old resentments flared up, too, against her parents and Richard. She pushed them down again, and went on. 'I write down as much as I can manage so it's there if I need it, but inevitably, no matter how hard I try, I slip up sometimes.'

'This is why you didn't want to work for me initially, and why you wanted me to accept Deborah in your place once you'd sorted things out for me a bit.' He stopped and raked a hand through his hair, and that awful, pitying glance was back on his face again. 'And it's why you're trying to push Deborah onto me again now.'

He continued. 'In terms of your work commitments to me, Lily, this changes nothing. I still need you as my secretary, in that chair every morning taking care of the workload. I need it now more than ever, as it happens.'

'Deborah will be a much better choice for you—'

He swore—a soft, sharp, eloquent word. 'Deborah doesn't know her way around the office, isn't familiar with it, with me and with my expectations and way of working. You're familiar with those things, Lily. Those things are locked into your head just fine.'

As though he expected her to argue the point, he held up a hand. 'We're already busy, and another project came to a head last night. It's a major deal. I need to look into it personally, and I need you with me while I do it. You, Lily. Not some clueless stranger.'

A part of her reached for the reprieve from leaving him—oh, foolish part that it was. If he needed her, couldn't she gain satisfaction from continuing to help him?

Before she could stop herself, she asked, 'What project, exactly?' Her hands shook as she opened her notebook and poised the pencil over it. Her gaze roved features that had become indelibly familiar, and far too dear. 'I'm just asking about the project. It doesn't mean I'll stay on, or have anything to do with it.'

His jaw clamped, but after a moment he took a folder from the briefcase that rested at his side. 'The project relates to a cartel of factory owners. They're looking for a financial partner to assist with a major expansion into the world-wide market. I had a brief phone conference with several of the head people about the idea a few months ago. Now they're ready to move on it, and I know I have to act quickly if I want in.'

He flipped the folder open to reveal a number of faxed pages, some with pictures of buildings on them. 'These are organics producers and their associated factories and farms. They deal in flours, nuts and grains mostly. There's also a confectionery factory.'

'They contacted you at home last night?' She guessed it from the different grade of fax paper in the folder, and from the fact that he had said nothing of it to her until now.

Then she reminded herself she couldn't be sure of that, and reached for her notebook to check back through the pages.

'This is the first you've heard of it.' He made the statement with that gentle tone in his voice again, and pushed the folder across the desk. As though it was nothing out of the ordinary to help her decide whether her memory had betrayed her or not.

She didn't know how to respond to that, and

finally settled on, 'Okay. Thank you.' To take her mind off that awkward feeling, she opened the folder and began to study the contents, only to feel compelled to look up again when she felt his gaze on her.

In his expression she caught a glimpse of some deep, banked emotion, before he blinked and looked away. Pity. It must have been pity.

Yet it hadn't looked quite like that. 'The factories are all really rural,' she observed. 'On farms and at the edges of small townships, by the looks of this.'

'Yes.' He leaned forward. 'What do you think are the chances of the project being viable?'

Perhaps it was the fact that his voice turned to one of challenge, as though he really wanted to hear her opinion. Or maybe she just wanted to prove herself, now that he knew her limitations.

She didn't know, but, despite herself, she said with conviction, 'I know you'd definitely be interested in this. From what's here, I think you could make money out of it.'

'That was my feeling, too.' He sat back in his chair. 'We need to leave later this morning to start our tour of the group of small farms and factories. We won't get back to Sydney until the weekend.'

And this was crunch point. Did she agree, or not agree? On the one hand, she would have him to herself for days out in the countryside, away from the demands of the office. She could bank up some memories, the kind that wouldn't leave her, but they would be of a boss-and-secretary nature. He felt nothing else for her now.

'We go to five different places.' He named each place, and flipped out a map that revealed the spread of the properties across parts of Victoria and New South Wales.

When he pointed to the final destination, she gave an involuntary start. *Albury-Wodonga.*

Actually, he said the factory was situated forty kilometres from the twin towns, and that their rental accommodation was set on a rural property not far from the factory. So it wasn't as if there would be any likelihood of Lily meeting up with her parents or Richard.

Zach gave her a frowning glance. 'Is there a problem?'

'No. It was just a random thought.' She drew a deep breath. 'I'd like to help you, Zach…'

'But you won't?' Before she could point out that she had been about to say she would do the work, his voice sharpened and his gaze hardened. 'I acknowledge things have changed, that they can never be the same between us now. But I didn't think you'd desert the ship when you have an obligation to stay with it. I thought you were stronger than that.'

Shock widened her eyes. So many emotions fought for space inside her that she felt quite faint. She had been a lot of things in the face of the damage to her memory, but, until now, no one had suggested weak was one of them.

'You thought I was stronger?' Her spine straightened, her chin pushed forward. She would *show* him that she was the opposite of weak, damn him. 'And I thought you were more intuitive than you apparently are, because you've missed what I was about to say completely.

'I *am* strong, Zach. I'm stronger than you'll ever imagine or know.' She bared her teeth in the semblance of a smile. 'You want me to work with you on this project? I'll do it. In fact, I'll work out the entire contract without a single complaint, just as you've wanted from the start!'

He had just better not blame her when he started to regret that she was still in his employ. 'Now, when do we leave for this trip?'

CHAPTER NINE

A PART of Zach wanted to treat Lily like the most fragile glass. To wrap her in cotton wool and carry her gently, so nothing could threaten even the least harm to her.

At first, Lily had been prickly and defensive after their talk at the coffee shop. It had taken hard work to see her relax again in his company.

And, all the while, his desire for her continued to torment him. He had thought the change in his knowledge of her had somehow ended her interest in him. The last day and a half had disproved that. She still wanted him, but was fighting to hide it.

Zach was tired of fighting the forces that drew him to her. His physical interest had developed into something so much more. He admired Lily more and more. He wanted to *show* her, in the best and most truthful way he knew how, just how special she was, even if he couldn't follow through with a long-term commitment. Maybe it was madness. He only knew he ached for her.

Lily examined the mass of licorice mixture in a vat at the final factory on their tour agenda. Zach watched her slender hands move as she tested the weight of the vat, and wanted to feel them caressing his chest, touching his face.

'It's heavy, isn't it? And that's just one small batch.' The owner grinned as they moved away.

'Let's take a look around, shall we?' Zach addressed his request to the owner, and Lily drew notebook and pencil from her bag.

The factory thrived in a concrete building with a large, built-on, hewn-log restaurant with windows overlooking a nearby creek. They moved from the receiving room to view the section of the factory where the flour was milled.

'It's a fully organic process from the day the wheat is planted to the day it ends up as flour here. We supply our flour to health food stores all over Australia. We also use it in our licorice, and in the cakes and some of the other products sold in the restaurant.' The owner showed them a handful of the grains.

Zach nodded, and hoped he looked more intelligent than he felt. Most of his brain space was taken up with noticing every move Lily made. She stepped closer to examine the wheat, and their arms brushed. Zach didn't quite manage to suppress a soft groan. Her gaze whipped to his and clung and, for once, the full strength of her desire for him shone through.

'I hadn't realised that flour was a key ingredient in licorice.' Lily looked at him, and confusion and questions shone in her eyes. Questions about *them*, not about this factory.

They continued their tour, and examined the tumbling machines that applied the many coats of fine chocolate to the licorice, before moving on to view the large restaurant kitchen. Lily continued to ask questions and take notes, but Zach caught the slight breathlessness in her voice and reacted, because he was under the same spell.

Later, as Zach examined a long conveyor belt used for cooling the confection items in the factory proper, he heard Lily's name called in a questioning tone.

'Lily Kellaway? It *is* you. I could have sworn your mother said you were out of the country.' A woman broke away from the group making their way past. 'Don't tell me you've moved back to Albury?'

'Hello, um, Michelle.' Lily took the woman's arm and drew her away, and the factory owner drew Zach's attention with a complicated rundown of the batch flow they managed on each of the different days in the confectionery part of the factory.

Zach tried to take in the facts and figures. He heard no more of Lily's conversation, but was aware of her every second until she joined him again.

When she did, he glanced at her strained face and, without thinking about it, wrapped his arm around her shoulders and hugged her against his side. 'Are you okay?'

She looked up as he bent down to ask the question. His words landed a breath away from her lips. His train of thought disintegrated. She seemed to lose track, too, her gaze fixed on his mouth. The owner had walked on ahead and they were momentarily alone.

Zach forced himself to release her, but stayed by her side, unable and unwilling to take even a few steps away from her. That single moment of vulnerability on her part, even though she hadn't explained it, added to so many others to unlock something inside Zach at last.

Feelings welled up in him that he couldn't explain, or even define, except to know that he wanted her to believe in herself, to regain her shaken confidence. His previous determination to be cautious towards her fled in the face of these feelings.

At the end of the tour, Zach left Lily browsing the gift shop and drew the owner aside.

Even as he walked away from Lily, his connection to her remained. He fixed his gaze on the owner, so he could impart the good news of his decision. 'As the last on the list, and the cartel's chosen leader, I know you've been on tenterhooks. I won't keep you waiting any longer. I'm happy with the figures provided by your accountant, and I'm more than impressed with all the factories, yours included. You'll receive my written offer within the next few days.'

The owner gave a whoop and pumped Zach's hand as he thanked him. Zach nodded, and excused himself so the man could go share his news. And, before he went back to Lily, he pondered. Why had she not mentioned that her family lived so close by? Surely she would want a chance to see them during her stay here? They rarely got together…

On impulse, he pulled out his cell phone. A call to the phone's information service, and another quick one, and he tucked the phone away and strode purposefully to join Lily as she laid claim to a bag bulging with goodies from the gift shop.

Outside, Zach handed Lily into the rental car in silence. It was that or snatch her close there and then and kiss her to oblivion.

'It was a good tour, the best factory of the bunch.' Her words were soft, and somehow hesitant, but also held that breathlessness that Zach felt inside himself.

'I told him I'll buy in.' One glance at her was nowhere near enough. He forced his gaze back to the road, but couldn't hold back any longer. 'I still want to make love to you, Lily. If you gave me the slightest sign that you were willing, I would follow through on that right now.'

Did Zach have any idea what he was saying? How it tempted Lily? She had wanted memories from this trip. Now Zach was letting her know that her condition *didn't* stop his desire for her. He wanted her even so. She must have been mistaken about his reaction at the coffee shop! Or perhaps he had just needed some time to adjust to the knowledge.

She gave way to the longing to be accepted just as she was. And she knew she would take this chance while she could. A chance to make love with him, just once, while they both wanted it, while they were here in the heart of the countryside. A time out of time. 'Then I'm giving you a sign, Zach. Please make love to me.'

'I will.' He pledged it, all other thoughts buried beneath this need.

Silence licked around them in tendrils of expectant heat as he drove them towards the secluded Manor House Restaurant Inn set on private acreage a few kilometres beyond the tiny town.

When they stopped in the parking lot beside the restored inn, with its gabled roof, sweeping verandas and high, mullioned windows, the blue of Lily's eyes had darkened almost to indigo. She fumbled with the catch of her door, but her words were steady and determined when she spoke. 'Let's go inside.'

He checked them in quickly. They climbed

the carved-wood staircase in silence. His heart raced when she moved unerringly to the door allocated to her, opened it with a trembling hand and pushed it wide.

In a heartbeat, he had shoved their luggage inside, freed his hands, and backed her into the room. He closed and locked the door behind them.

'Lily. Beautiful, wonderful Lily.' He kissed the side of her face, the shell of her ear, and revelled in the shudder that coursed through her.

'You're a very special woman. I want to show you how much I mean that.' He kissed her so long and so deeply that he almost lost himself. When he finally drew back, they were both panting, trembling.

Her arms snaked upward to twine around his neck.

Zach drew a ragged breath. 'I want to hold you as close to me as I can. I want to touch you and explore you and learn you.'

She moaned and closed her eyes. Outside, an owl hooted. The country sound gave this moment a feeling of being something out of reality. Zach pushed the thought aside. How could this be any more real?

When her hands reached for the buttons of

his shirt, he held her gaze and felt the blaze of heat as her fingers worked to bare his chest. He shrugged the shirt away and clenched his teeth as she touched him, then leaned forward to press her mouth against his hot skin.

'You're going to kill me.' It seemed perfectly natural to tell her so. And equally right to draw her knit shirt from the waistband of her jeans and tug it over her head.

The freckles didn't go beyond her shoulders. The skin below was creamy white, soft and fragrant. With a deep groan, he buried his face in her neck, then after a moment dipped his head to trace the cleft between her breasts with his lips.

'I need you.' He could barely manage to say even that much. His hands tightened on her shoulders, stroked upward and into her hair.

She moved her hands across his back. 'I need you, too.'

'Give me your mouth. Please.' A harsh command, a begging request. Then he simply swooped, his heart hammering, every thought focussed on having her, giving to her, bringing them together.

Her lips melded to his in a fit so lush, so perfect, his entire body thrummed. His heart beat fiercely, and a well of something deep and agonising rose up.

She's the only one who can answer this feeling. The only one...

'Come to bed with me.' Her soft words wrapped around him, warmed him with sensual promise as her gaze met his, her eyes shimmering with unspoken feelings. 'Let's not think. Let's just be together.'

Zach breathed her name as he joined her on the bed. His arms found their way naturally around her as though they, and his body, had been made for this, for holding her, for being with her.

Yet her words stayed with him—because he *wasn't* thinking, was instead reacting fully with his senses, and what if that wasn't the right thing to do? What if Lily somehow expected more from him than that?

The thoughts came then, reminders of Lily's unwillingness to be intimate without commitment. He had started this for good reasons, but those reasons would not be enough for her later.

She stroked her hands across his back and shoulders, and onto his chest. 'Hold me, Zach. Just...hold me.'

'Yes.' He told himself this was fine, but, try as he might, he couldn't ignore those internal warnings. He wanted to, but he couldn't. Because he couldn't share in the emotional commitment that should be part of it.

Lily deserved all that and nothing less.

His arms stiffened as he confronted what he was doing far too late, where it would lead them, and the hurt that would follow if he let this happen.

This would hurt her anyway, and he tried to soften his words as he forced his arms to let her go. 'I'm sorry. I shouldn't have started this. I wanted to ignore what I know of you, but it is part of you.' It wasn't wrong for her to want commitment in an intimate relationship. It was right. But Zach couldn't give her that. 'The way you are won't change, and unfortunately I can't, either…'

His words petered out, stilled by the look of deep hurt in her eyes. With her lips pressed together and her eyes forced wide, as though if she let them relax they would reveal far too much, she shifted away from him and climbed from the bed.

'We got carried away. It was just desire.' She moved into the sitting room, drew a wrap from her travel bag, and slipped her arms into it. 'I wish I hadn't let things get this far, either!'

He silently dressed too. 'I can't give you what you need, Lily.' How he wished it was different. 'The depth of commitment and time someone like you would have to have.' *A woman made for loving and being loved in return.*

She gave a shrug that cut right to his heart. 'Caring about me would be too high-maintenance for you. I get it.'

Her words held a tremble that made him want to kick himself all the way back to Sydney, and keep on kicking. Disappointment and hurt still lurked in her eyes.

All he could do was stay silent, because he *couldn't* maintain a relationship with her. His commitment to his family would tear it down, just as had happened once before. 'I wish things could be different.'

'Oh, I'm sure you do.' Mouth pinched, she lifted her chin and held her shoulders back. 'But things aren't different. I'd like you to leave now, please. I want to be alone.'

There was nothing he could do. Zach gathered his travel bag and let himself out the door.

CHAPTER TEN

'HAS Ms Kellaway left her room yet?' Zach stood in the reception foyer and asked the question of the cheery Manor House owner who stood behind the old-fashioned check-in counter. Zach wanted to dislike the guy, simply because he looked happy.

'I believe so, but allow me to try the room.' The man reached for the phone.

'Thanks.' Last night gnawed at Zach. The knowledge that he had hurt Lily concerned him most of all, but something else gnawed at him, too. He had made a phone call yesterday on the spur of the moment while Lily had browsed the gift shop at the confectionery factory. Snap decisions weren't his usual style, but he had made one and acted on it. Now he had to tell Lily about it.

Surely she would welcome a face-to-face

meeting with her parents? So why did he feel so uneasy about it now?

Because you know you've hurt her. You should have left her alone.

Yes…

He sensed her presence a moment before the owner's gaze moved beyond him, and the man returned the phone to its cradle.

Zach turned. There were shadows under Lily's eyes, and in them. His stomach tightened as he acknowledged he had caused those shadows. 'I tried your room before I came down, but there was no response.'

'I went for a walk along the creek. The kookaburras gave a morning chorus for me from the gum trees. I'd forgotten what that sounded like.' Strain rasped in her voice. The same strain he felt inside, but she was putting on a valiant effort at normality. 'I'm ready to leave any time you like.'

'You've eaten already?' He had to forget wanting and needing her. For both their sakes, he had to forget.

She folded her arms. 'I haven't eaten, but I don't mind waiting until we get to the airport.'

All her barriers were up again, only this time it was worse. 'I invited your parents to have breakfast with us this morning.' He could see no other way to tell her, and the older couple should be here any minute. 'I thought you might enjoy a chance to see them. I meant to tell you yesterday afternoon, but it slipped my mind.'

His thoughts had been wrapped up in her.

At his announcement, her face closed up. She drew a sharp breath. 'How do you even know?'

'That they live in Albury-Wodonga? I heard the woman from the tour group say so yesterday.' He had only half tuned in to the conversation, but had heard that much before they'd moved out of range. 'It prompted me to try to give you some time with your family.'

'I'm not useless and incapable of expressing the desire to fit a visit with my parents into our schedule.' Her low words struck out at him. 'If I'd wanted to do it, I would have.'

'I've made a mistake, haven't I? I'm sorry. After last night—'

'Last night has no bearing on anything.' She kept her voice low, but each word rejected him. 'We both got carried away by desire when we should have controlled it. But you've made it clear you didn't really want even a one-night stand with me, and I hope I've made my opinion clear now, too. Anything we thought we had is finished.'

'I stopped to protect *you*, Lily.'

'Whatever you say.' She obviously didn't want to believe him. 'Well? Where's this breakfast taking place?' Her face tipped up and her mouth firmed. She stalked towards the dining room. 'We're meeting them here, I assume?'

'That's right.' He watched her move to a table for four, choose a chair and sit in it, her back ramrod-straight.

Zach cautiously took his own seat beside her. He had only just done so when a middle-aged couple entered the dining room and quickly scanned it. When they spotted Lily and Zach seated side by side, they hurried over.

'Mr Swift. How nice of you to invite us to join you.' Lily's mother, thin, well-kept and…hard-looking… allowed her husband to seat her to Zach's left at the table. 'You must call me Dorothea, and my husband is Carl.'

'And I'm Zach.' He forced a smile, disconcerted by that rigid edge in the older woman. Physical similarities to Lily were there. They shared the same slim build, the same straight nose. Both had blue eyes, but Lily's were usually warm. Dorothea's seemed curiously devoid of life.

Lily's father, round-framed glasses perched high on the bridge of his nose, gave Zach a thoughtful examination. Her father wore his grey beard and hair cropped close, and was tall with slightly stooped shoulders. He shook Zach's hand. 'I've read about a number of your success stories. You've dealt with quite a few influential and important people.'

Zach returned their greetings, but his attention was fixed on Lily's silent presence beside him as the small but salient facts began to sink in.

Her parents had taken their seats without more than a glance in her direction. No hellos. No, *it's wonderful to see you.*' No kisses, no hugs. They had greeted *him*, and ignored their daughter. Why?

'Hello, Dad. Mum.' Lily's carefully controlled voice revealed no feeling. 'You both look well.'

'Run ragged with the usual volunteer work, but we're keeping our heads above water.' Her mother dispensed the response, and turned to Zach again. 'We do our best to be community-minded, you know.'

'A trait your daughter appears to have inherited.' He said it without inflection while his mind grappled with the realisation that her parents appeared more interested in him, and in themselves, than in Lily.

His conversation with Lily about last night hung over him, too, unresolved and uncomfortable. He wished they could be alone to maybe try to discuss things further. But then, what good would that do? Nothing had changed. 'Lily, too, is an active volunteer.'

'Really?' Dorothea Kellaway seemed to flounder. 'Well, I'm sure that's very nice.'

After an awkward pause, Lily's mother turned to her. 'Where do you volunteer? Is it any place that would know of, er, that would know your family?'

'I volunteer at the brain institute that helped with my rehabilitation after I moved to Sydney.' Lily's gaze was guarded, but also challenging.

Zach saw the pain in the backs of her eyes, and the spark of rebellious anger before she spoke again. 'I also run my own temp secretary agency, which is why I'm working for Zach at the moment. None of this has ever been a secret.'

'Well, we're always so busy when we

phone you.' Her mother toyed with the edge of the table cloth. 'If there'd been more time to talk, perhaps—'

'You mean when I phone you.' Lily corrected gently. 'It's funny how things can get confused. Like some of my old friends thinking I'd moved overseas.' She looked away, but not before Zach saw her swallow hard.

Her mother had told people she was out of the country? It didn't take a genius to add it up. Her father hadn't said much, but this woman who called herself Lily's mother was ashamed of her! Zach's fists clenched beneath the table as he fought to control his reaction, his fury.

Lily's father cast a suspicious glance in his wife's direction.

'Well, I'd thought you might like to travel.' Dorothea almost snapped the words at her daughter. 'You didn't want the sanatorium, but your father and I set up an allowance so you wouldn't have to expose yourself.'

'But I've looked after myself. I haven't needed your allowance, or to be locked away.' Lily's low words brought a tight look to her mother's face before the older woman shifted her gaze.

'Let's order.' Lily's father spoke hurriedly.

A mixture of emotions stormed through Zach. Regret. Anger. Pride and fury. This wretched meeting was at his instigation, and the knowledge sat hard with him. Could he make things *any* worse for Lily?

'How is your agency going, Lilybell?' Her father raised his menu and buried his nose in it, but looked at her over the top with what might have been regret.

Lily lifted her menu, too, and her face softened as she looked at her father. 'It's flourishing.'

'Hmm. Well, I'm glad.' He disappeared into his menu again, thus avoiding a glare from his wife.

Dorothea plucked the menu wordlessly and rudely from Lily's hands, and Zach's gaze narrowed once again.

The waitress appeared.

Lily's chest rose and fell in shallow breaths, and Zach thought he could just, quite possibly, be on the verge of committing a crime of violence. Wringing Dorothea Kellaway's neck held a certain appeal.

Zach leaned towards Lily on a well of fierce protectiveness and deep regret. He set his lips against her ear. 'Let me end this. We'll just go.'

'No.' Steel threaded the single word. 'I'm not a coward.'

Dorothea hustled out her order to the waitress. 'And you can bring toast and a glass of water for Lily.'

Lily smiled nicely for the waitress as she turned to her. 'Actually, I'd like a pot of tea, yoghurt and stewed fruit, and toast and marmalade. Do you have low-fat French vanilla yoghurt?'

'Yes, we have that.' The waitress returned the smile and made a note on her order pad.

After a disapproving hesitation, her mother subsided.

Lily's father made his order in a subdued voice. Zach barely noticed, because he was seething so deeply it was all he could do to breathe normally and not start breaking things. He hadn't realised he had gripped Lily's hand beneath the table until she made a soft gasping sound and pulled it away.

'Toast. Bacon and eggs. Coffee. Juice.' He bit the words out, and made sure he gave the waitress eye contact to let her see he wasn't angry with her. 'Thank you. As quickly as you can manage it would be helpful.'

'So, Mr and Mrs Kellaway. How do you

pass your time in Albury-Wodonga?' He'd forget calling them by their first names. They'd done nothing to warrant familiarity—quite the opposite, as far as Zach was concerned! 'Aside from your charitable works, that is?'

His jaw clamped, but words emerged through his clenched teeth. 'It's clear you haven't followed Lily's progress at all, which astounds me, considering she's forged a brilliant new career for herself in Sydney.'

'Zach.' Lily stiffened her spine even more than she already had.

Her father cleared his throat. 'I hold a management position at Towers University. Lily studied psychology there before—'

'I support Carl, of course.' Lily's mother quickly jumped in. 'A good man needs a strong woman behind him. We have quite a position in the community, you understand.' A tinkling laugh followed this pronouncement. 'One has to work to achieve such respect, but we don't mind, do we, dear?'

The food arrived. Lily's mother watched her eat her fruit and yoghurt as though she expected one or both to explode out of her bowl at any second.

Zach pushed his food around his plate, and

wanted to stop all pretence of civility. He wanted to confront these people openly and utterly, and make them account for their behaviour towards their daughter.

For Lily's sake, he stuck with stilted, tedious small talk while the guilt for making this happen ate at him.

The moment the meal ended, he got to his feet, and took Lily's elbow in a tender hold that he hoped expressed the regret he couldn't yet speak out loud.

As she rose in response to his guiding grip, he offered a stiff nod to the two who remained seated at the table. 'We need to go. Lily and I can see ourselves off, so please don't get up. Finish your meal.'

'Goodbye, Mum.' Lily's gaze searched her mother's face before she turned to look at her father. Her expression softened a little. 'Bye, Dad. It was good to see you.'

Zach respected and admired her all the more just then as she gave her parents such courtesy. He managed not to express the wish that their remaining breakfast choke them. Instead he nodded, and hustled Lily out of the room.

The accommodation was pre-paid. Their bags waited at the ready for them. Zach passed

several large bills to the owner. 'For the restaurant costs, if you wouldn't mind settling it
once our guests leave. Please keep the change.'

A bag in each hand, he led the way towards
the hire car. With each step, the fury he had
suppressed during the meal rose. Those
people, who called themselves her parents,
treated Lily like an embarrassment. Particularly her mother, but her father shouldn't
hide in silence while it happened.

His Lily.

They had apparently done so from the day
her brain had been damaged, and somehow
Zach doubted they had *ever* been particularly
effusive in showing their love to her.

'You're twice as smart, innovative and
capable as most people I could name.' He
gritted the words as he flung their luggage into
the back of the car and rounded it to get into
the driver's side. 'They should acknowledge
that fact!'

Lily climbed inside the car, too. 'What right
have you got to say anything?'

She was right, but her parents should be
shouting her praise from the rooftops, and
showing people how proud they were of her.
If she were his to keep, to have and to hold—

His breath caught as he realised the significance of those thoughts, and the long-term commitment they suggested. Well, if he had Lily in that way, if that miracle somehow happened—which it never would—he would praise her and be proud of her, and so much more.

Because he didn't trust his emotions, he subsided into tense silence.

They were halfway to the airport before Zach calmed down enough to notice that Lily was still silent too. He immediately turned off the road onto a tree-shrouded laneway and stopped the car. An apology was nowhere near enough, but he had to express his regret.

'I'm completely at fault for what happened back there.' He wanted to take her hand in his, but knew if he tried she would probably reject him again. So he told her the truth, and hoped it would go some way towards healing the fresh wound of this morning's meeting. 'Aside from last night, I can't think of a time when I've disliked myself more.'

Every word felt inadequate, but he pushed on. 'I should have asked if you'd like to see them. If I'd thought about the fact that you didn't speak of them much, I might have realised…'

His words trailed off, and he sought her gaze with a searching glance. 'I don't expect you to forgive me for arranging that episode, but I am sorry.'

She turned her head away, fixed her gaze at a point beyond her window. Her voice was flat. 'It's not as if their attitude is anything unusual.' Her face closed into a determined mask, and she turned her head to look back the way they had come. 'We should get back on the road. It wouldn't do to be late to the airport.'

Zach turned the car back onto the road, but his thoughts were still on their conversation. On all that had happened, and on the growing realisation of how much Lily truly had been forced to come to terms with.

Her mother had tried to hide her away in a sanatorium. If Lily had complied, would she still be there today, while her mother swanned about the place pretending her daughter didn't exist?

Zach wanted to take Lily straight to *his* mother. To give her the same love from Anne that had sustained him through the grief of losing his father, and through his fears about being able to hold up in his dad's footsteps.

He wanted to give Lily *family*. The one thing that had torn his life apart when he'd tried to commit to a woman.

At the airport, they separated briefly while he signed off on the use of the hired car. When he joined her again, it was to queue for their boarding passes and to check their luggage in. Lily didn't speak, but tension radiated from her. He didn't feel any better.

Memories of last night came back full-force as he absorbed her closeness, and with those memories came regret so deep he couldn't fathom it.

Zach acknowledged his confusion. Despite everything, he didn't ever want Lily to leave his life. He couldn't see his days without her there, part of them. Her sticky notes on his computer. Her forwarded reminders popping up in his email inbox just in time for her to come and tell him the same information when she retrieved it from her diary.

He cared for her. Too much. Too intensely. In ways he didn't want to examine. And it was all utterly hopeless, because he didn't have enough to give her. A few left-over crumbs of his life, after he'd handed the rest to his family and his job.

CHAPTER ELEVEN

'I'LL get some coffee. Do you want any?' Lily made the excuse because she needed a moment away from Zach.

'Nothing for me, thanks.' He let her go without protest.

Yet, as she walked away, she felt his gaze on her. Perhaps he was still angry over her parents' behaviour.

Well, she was angry, too. At him, *and* at her parents. Lily had been angry with her mum and dad for a long time. She hadn't realised the whole truth of that until this morning. They *should* have been there for her. Not just after her accident, but right through her life.

But Zach had rejected her, too, and then gone on to act as though *he* had a right to do that but her parents didn't.

While she waited for her coffee, Lily pulled

out her cell phone to call Deborah, hoping just
to hear her friend's calm, rational voice. There
was no answer. As she disconnected, their
flight was called.

After taking two sips of the coffee, she abandoned the rest into a trash bin. She joined Zach,
and they made their way to the boarding area.
Zach had just stepped through when she
thought she heard her name called, and hesitated.

Several people filed past her and she looked
back, and instantly recognised the man hur-
rying towards her. *'Richard.'*

He stopped so close to her that she could
have touched him. She hadn't heard from him
for twelve months, and suddenly here he was.
How had he even known to find her here?
What did he want?

'Lily. I understand from your parents that
you're here with Zachary Swift.' His glance
searched around her, behind her. 'I'd like to
meet him.'

This was the man she had once pledged to
marry. The man who had insisted she go
kayaking in white water that day, despite her
lack of experience, despite her protests.

Resentment stirred, but her life was what it

was. And Richard was just a selfish, self-gratifying man who would have made her miserable.

In truth, she was well out of the relationship, and relieved beyond measure to know that he no longer made her feel anything but a rather abstract pity for the shallowness that lurked behind his pseudo-charming exterior.

'Did my mother put you up to this?' The moment she asked the question, she knew it was true. But why?

She let her gaze rove him indifferently, and said in calm, almost disinterested tones, 'I'm very well, Richard. My work is prospering. I'm in good health, all things considered. Thank you for asking.'

'You sound almost normal.' This fact appeared to confuse him. 'Where's your employer?' He all but snapped his fingers. 'Get him back here before your flight leaves. I want a word with him. I—' He cut himself off. 'I mean, the *university* could do with some funding, particularly in my area. It's a golden opportunity…'

'Ah.' So Richard wanted to meet the *prestigious* Zachary Swift. The man with money and connections who might give him a donation that would aid his climb through the ranks of university staff.

Richard was as bad as her mother, viewing everyone through a lens coloured by his desire to get to the top.

'My boss deals in the business of buying companies, and buying into companies. If you have one on your hands and need a buyer or a partner, make an appointment like everyone else.' She felt her lip curl in derision. 'Otherwise, stay away from us.'

The final boarding call came over the intercom. She turned and saw Zach paused, waiting for her, his gaze watchful, the rest of his face a blank mask.

She turned back to her ex-fiancé's angry face, and wondered how she could have been so blind about him. But, sadly, she already knew the answer. She had wanted to please her parents, and had tried not to see Richard's selfishness and his other faults. They had come home to roost the day he'd realised she would never get her full brain function back. Clearly, he hadn't improved with the passage of time!

An airline official approached. 'Ma'am? Are you taking this flight, or staying behind?'

'I'm taking it.' She turned away from Richard and moved towards Zach.

The flight was short, and Lily and Zach ended up seated in separate parts of the plane because of some mix-up with the boarding passes. Lily didn't mind. She welcomed the time away from Zach to try to pull her thoughts and emotions together.

When they arrived at Sydney airport, it hummed with noise. The moment Zach turned his cell phone back on inside the terminal, it rang.

'I'll get a luggage trolley.' Lily left him to stand beside their bags and answer his call.

When she came back with a trolley, she heard him address the caller as 'Steele', and knew it was a call from his finance manager.

'Is it really necessary for me to handle this problem right now?' Zach tossed their luggage onto the trolley, and started pushing it one-handed as he scowled into the phone.

Lily moved along beside him. She had told Zach she would work out her contract to the end. But would he still want that now, after all that had happened? Pride wouldn't allow her to ask again to leave.

'Why are Gunterson and Greig so upset?

We got the proposal to them on time, and they sounded quite positive about the deal.' Zach's hand clenched around the cell phone and his voice harshened. 'Surely, whatever problem it is, it can wait until Monday?'

Steele talked on for another minute. Then Zach ended the call and snapped the phone shut.

Lily turned to him. 'What's wrong?'

'It's the Mulligan project.' He grimaced, and shoved the trolley faster as they approached the building's exit doors. 'They're thinking of pulling out.'

'What do you need to do to fix the problem?'

He gave a flat laugh. 'Wine them, dine them. Convince them they're the most important project I have on my books.'

Even if they weren't, but in fact the Mulligan project was worth a lot of money.

They made their way into the taxi queue and began the slow shift forward. Stop, start, stop, start.

Zach handled their luggage without seeming to even think about it. 'In my absence, Gunterson and Greig have gone cold on our proposal. Despite Steele's efforts, they refuse to talk to him or explain the reason for their change of heart. The deal was all but sewn up, and now I'm going to have to try to get it back to that position.'

And suddenly Lily had a focus, *and* a way to prove herself. To show she could just go on, no matter what had happened between them. No matter that Zach hadn't been able to make love to her in the face of her disability. She seized the chance to direct her thoughts towards fixing this business problem.

'What about a long lunch meeting with drinks and lots of table talk? Right now—today? Given that it's the weekend, and they'll know you're sacrificing your time for them, something like that might be your best bet.'

'That's a good idea.' He hesitated for just a moment. 'The lunch would go a lot better if you were there.'

She cautioned herself to remember that his invitation meant nothing at all, personally. Even so, she wanted to believe he still valued her *somehow*, even if only as his temporary secretary. 'You really think my presence would be of some help?'

'Yes. I'll bet you could think of a great place for the lunch, too.' He reminded her about her

galloping garçon efforts that first day at work.
'Something good like that would get them in
the right mood.'

Although they spoke of business matters,
Zach's gaze on her held awareness, regret,
hunger. Would it ever end—this heart-deep
longing she felt for him?

'How many people work for the Mulligan
operation?' She tucked her bottom lip in while
she considered his request.

'Five hundred workers with specialised
skills they won't be able to use elsewhere.'

'That's a lot of people and jobs. Why don't
we book a venue right now? In fact, why not
that fabulous cliff-top restaurant overlooking
Whale Beach?'

Zach nodded and flipped open his phone once
again, and Lily assured herself she could do
this, could maintain her self-control for one
short afternoon, and not fall prey again to the
need that had swept her up during their trip
away.

'The afternoon went well, I think. There's
something to be said for setting.' Lily made the
comment as they emerged from the taxi
outside her apartment in the late afternoon.

Nerves pulled at her, and she struggled to ignore them.

'It was as successful as we could have hoped.' Zach drew out her travel bag and leaned in to ask the driver to wait, then turned back to her. His hair was wind-tousled. When he stepped close to her, she could smell sea air on his clothes and in his hair. 'In large part due to you choosing that venue.'

'I know it cost you a lot of dollars. I'm very easy with your money, aren't I?' She wasn't really worried about that. He would have vetoed it if he'd disliked the idea. But she *was* uneasy, now that the day was over. What would happen next? 'I'd heard how beautiful the views were by sea plane over Sydney Harbour, but that's the first time I'd seen them from that perspective.'

'Yes. Very lovely.' But Zach's gaze rested on her face, and a chord resonated within her at the intensity of that look.

This afternoon, at times when she'd caught his gaze on her, it had seemed like he desired her and more. Oh, she was so confused! They walked to her front door, and he put the bag down. When he looked at her, she simply wanted to melt into his arms again. Why was it so easy for her to lose sight of all that had happened between them?

'Palm Beach and Whale Beach are both so beautiful, too. The Norfolk Island pines and that blue, blue water. The long stretches of golden sand and palm trees.' She forced the words to a stop.

But the few hours, despite being primarily for business purposes, had held a forbidden magic for her.

The views from the cliff-top restaurant windows. The feeling of Zach at her side through the afternoon. His hand clasped around hers as he helped her alight from the sea plane. The lapping of the sea beneath their feet as they'd walked the wharf towards the waiting restaurant car.

And that long, silent walk on the beach while they'd given their guests some space and time to discuss their options in private. Tension had buzzed between them, but she had soaked up that time together and tried not to think ahead.

'You looked beautiful with the sea behind you, and nothing but endless sand beneath your feet.' His voice was deep and hungry.

He seemed to realise it at the same time she did.

'I hope Gunterson and Greig's delegates will push ahead with the deal, now.' The key eluded her as she dug around in her purse.

'Whether they do or not, I'm glad I had you with me today. I doubt things would have worked out half as well without you there.'

Just as she found the key, his hand closed over hers. He lifted her hand and kissed her fingertips. Only that, but she wanted to cry.

Their gazes caught and held, and his mouth brushed hers while her heart cried *yes*, even as *she* cried no.

'No, Zach.'

He made a harsh sound. Turned his head away. 'You'll stay with me to the end of the contract.' He made it a statement.

She tipped her chin in confirmation. 'Like I said, I'm not a coward. But please go now, Zach. It's been a draining few days, and this isn't helping.'

His fists tightened at his sides and a flare of something dark washed across his face. 'There are things I want, no, *need* to know about what happened to you. I feel as though you're blaming that somehow for what happened back at the inn.'

'I don't know what you mean.' Inside the

house, Jemima must have become aware of Lily's presence and started to howl loudly, adding to the general feeling of cacophony resonating within her.

The luncheon aside, last night and this morning had been tough. She had to be tougher. 'I'll see you at work on Monday.'

She took up her travel bag and used it to encourage Jemima backward into the house when she opened the door. A moment later, the door was closed and locked behind her, and Zach's footsteps were receding down the path.

Zach left Lily because she'd made it clear she was at the end of her endurance, but questions remained unresolved in his head. He didn't think he would be able to rest until he had answers to those questions.

Just how bad had things been for her as a result of her injury? How exactly had it happened? *Was* she blaming her condition somehow for the fact that he had stopped their lovemaking? If so, she had misunderstood him.

She still seemed fragile when she arrived at work Monday morning, so Zach kept his distance, although he couldn't prevent his gaze from honing in on her often as she worked away at her desk.

Partway through the afternoon, she stepped into his office to leave a stack of typed letters for him to sign, and he looked up and caught her gaze on him. Wariness pooled in her eyes, and Zach knew he *had* to have those answers *now*, whether she felt ready or not. 'You never told me, you know. How did your accident happen? That was your ex-fiancé at the airport, wasn't it? I heard you say his name. Why did he leave you, Lily? Why didn't he stay by your side and help you through what had happened to you? Why did he come to the airport to see you?'

'My mother contacted Richard.' Lily said it in a flat tone that still somehow managed to convey a sense of hurt. 'He came to the airport in the hopes of meeting you.'

'Me? Why?' This wasn't the answer Zach had expected. 'What could he possibly want from me?'

'Money.' Lily shrugged her slender shoulders. She seemed almost embarrassed as she went on. 'A grant, I think, which would make him look good and help him climb the ranks at the university. My father used to support him financially. I thought he still did, but maybe he doesn't.'

Zach curled his hands into fists. 'What did you tell Richard when you spoke to him?' *Was that all he wanted from you?*

A small smile hovered around the edges of her mouth. 'I told him to stay away from you, from me, and from this business. I think he got the message.'

Zach's mouth lifted, too, before he sobered. 'You don't…still have feelings for him?'

'No…' She didn't sound entirely certain.

Zach stood and moved towards her. 'Surely you must know how you feel?'

'I don't care about him.' Her fingers trembled as she raised her hand to brush her hair back from her face. 'I guess I feel guilty.'

Zach leaned forward in a protective move he couldn't prevent. 'Why? I can't imagine you've done anything to harm him.'

'I feel guilty because I've blamed him for my accident, and everything that followed.' She dropped her gaze, long lashes covering her expressive eyes.

A warning rumble started in Zach's throat. If Richard had hurt Lily in any way… He kept his voice deliberately gentle. 'Was there a reason for you to blame him? Tell me what happened.'

Her gaze rose again. 'Richard organised a

kayaking trip with some business associates he wanted to impress. They were all experienced, and he wanted his fiancée there to add to his status in their eyes. I told him I had no experience and didn't want to go, but he insisted.

'When we got into white water I realised I couldn't cope. I tried to paddle to the bank but I lost control, went under and hit my head on a submerged rock. The doctors at the hospital told me later that my brain had bounced inside my skull. I was unconscious when two of Richard's companions fished me out, during the rescue mission, and for some time after. If those people and the doctors hadn't acted so quickly and taken such care of me, I'd have died.'

Her eyes darkened with suppressed memories. 'Later, I blamed Richard. I've been blaming him for a long time, but I realise now that I can't blame him. He shouldn't have insisted I go, that's true, but it was my responsibility to say no and insist he make the trip without me.'

'I'll kill him with my bare hands.' Zach muttered an expletive beneath his breath. He stared at Lily, and wanted to hunt Richard down. 'It was at least partly his fault. The man was irresponsible—'

'Yes, I know.' She smiled as she cut him off. 'But ultimately I was in charge of myself. The accident happened because I made a poor choice.'

'Did you break up with him because you blamed him?' He could understand that, and he still wanted to pound on the guy. But he also wanted to comfort Lily, and he reached for her hands, holding them tight as he waited for her answer.

Lily shook her head. 'Richard didn't come to the hospital for almost a week. When he finally turned up, it was to tell me he couldn't remain engaged to someone who would never regain the full use of her brain. My parents rejected me as well. They wanted to hide me away somewhere so they didn't have to face what had happened to me. It hurt so much, Zach.'

Something inside his chest ripped apart. His voice was hoarse when he spoke. 'He didn't deserve you, Lily, and if that's the best your parents can do they don't deserve you, either.'

She tilted her head back to look into his eyes, her breath catching as their gazes locked. 'I've had so much anger inside me. I don't want to be like that. I want to live my life—to embrace everything and not be afraid.'

'You've been incredible and strong and amazing, in the face of the kind of odds that would wipe some people out completely.' That was what Zach saw. He groaned. That tide of feeling that had begun to well inside him earlier rose up again. 'If there's any guilt, forgive yourself and put it behind you.'

He looked down into her eyes, and he could only want her. *This Lily. His* Lily.

'Why are you doing this to me, Zach?' Lily's question was fraught with pain. 'You act as thought you want me, hunger for me, and all I want is to yield to that like I did before. But my memory loss is repugnant to you. I was there when you rejected me at the Manor House Inn, remember? Please don't do that to me again.'

'No, it's not like that.' He hugged her against his chest, held her there as he tried to convey the wrongness of her words to her through his touch.

Slowly, carefully, he held her at arms' length. 'I don't give a single damn about the state of your memory, other than to hate that it causes you pain. When have I ever said otherwise, or even led you to believe it?'

'But you pushed me away.' Confusion

clouded her eyes, but now there were other emotions to be seen in her gaze and expression as well. Soft, hesitant emotions that wrapped around his heart and squeezed.

'We intended to make love, and both of us knew it wouldn't turn into anything more than a night together in that rural setting so far away from all we know here. But you still stopped.' She drew a soft breath. 'It can only be because of my condition.'

'Maybe I shouldn't have stopped, because your condition had nothing to do with it, Lily. Nothing at all.' He growled the words, and then he went on. 'I stopped that night because I didn't want to hurt you by ending it after that. And all I did was make it worse, didn't I? At least, if we'd shared that, you'd have been sure of how much I desire you just as you are.

'I want to make love to you more than I've ever wanted anything in my life. I want to hold you and show you that you're wonderful. I care about you, Lily. More than I should. I wish I could give you the world.' He took a deep breath. 'I guess I didn't do a very good job of expressing empathy that day at the coffee shop. I hurt for you, and didn't know how to help you, and you were so prickly about it.'

She stared at him, and her breath caught on a sob of sound. 'Then make love to me now, Zach. Right now, so I *can* believe you desire me enough to do that.' She said it softly, and her eyes burned with both hunger and vulnerability. 'You can't give me the world. I know that. But give me this.'

The decision was made deep inside him before he could even consider standing against it. He tugged her into the outer office, snatched up her bag and pressed it into her hands. 'This time there'll be no going back for either of us. You understand that?'

'I understand.' She tipped that lovely chin again, looked into his eyes. Let him see the desire that fired her expression. 'Take me somewhere we can be alone.'

Take me... Emotion bubbled through Zach. Lily's revelations, the pain caused by her parents, her guilt over blaming Richard, all added up to make him *have* to prove to her that he found her utterly attractive, appealing on every level. 'There are things I want to show you—in my heart—I want, I need—'

'I want and need, too, so many things with you. I never expected to tell anybody how much it hurt me to lose my parents' support, and to wrestle with the guilt of blaming Richard for everything that happened.' She said it softly, and slipped her bag over her shoulder then headed for the door. 'Somehow, telling you those things has freed me, and I know now that I want this with you, just once. So *show* me, Zach.'

As on the night of his birthday party, he had her elbow in his grasp before she knew what was happening. He kissed her in the empty elevator. Pressed her against the cold, steel wall and ravaged her mouth, her face, her neck. And then his kisses softened, and he worshipped her slowly, tenderly, as his heart ached for her.

Lily wrapped her arms around him and held him as he counted the minutes until he had her in his bed.

His bed, because nothing else would do. Not for her. Not for him. Not for this.

The lift opened directly into the underground parking lot. They crossed to his car with a very circumspect distance of several feet between them. The area was deserted. He guided her to the car, and in the dim-lit silence he pulled her close again. Pressed against her. Kissed her again.

'Where are you taking me?' She asked it when they finally sat side by side on the leather seats. Her question underlined her acceptance that this would happen now, with the inevitability of the changing of the seasons or the ticking of a clock.

That powerful knowledge raced through him. He started the car and forced himself not to rush his movements. 'I'm taking you to my house, my bed.'

'Good. I want to be there.' She tossed her bag onto the floor of the car with an air of acceptance, and her hands came to rest, lightly clasped, against her thigh.

Zach covered those hands with one of his own, then reluctantly let go.

The drive to his home took time, and that time could have defused the heat and emotion that had brought them both to this point.

Instead, each silent moment, each breath she took, each breath he took, seemed to just make more of it.

Until he finally said, on the brink of madness as they arrived outside his house, 'If I don't have you, I'll die.'

'If I don't have you, I might very well die too.' Her laugh was half sob.

CHAPTER TWELVE

As Zach strode through his house, pulling Lily along by the hand, his destination and intent clear, Lily blurted one breathless concern. 'Daniel. You said he drops by here a lot.'

'He's at school, and he never comes here during working hours.' He pushed a door open and drew her into a cool, quiet room.

His room.

He reached for her, but, instead of tugging her forward with the demand that raged through him, he held her gently. Drew her to him gently.

'Your brother is a wonderful boy.' Zach had a family in the truest sense of the word. Maybe today, as they shared these moments, Lily could pretend just briefly that she was a part of that, too. Oh, what was she saying— thinking?

'A brother who can get the sulks as well as the next person, and, if you think small talk is going to make me forget how much I want you, you're wrong.' He buried his face in her hair and took a long, unsteady breath.

He kissed the crown of her head and caressed her shoulders, and shifted his gaze to look deep into her eyes. 'I can't ever be other than who and what I am, Lily. Even knowing that, I don't think I can walk away from this. I want you and need you too much.'

'I'm not asking you to stop, or trying to distract you. I know this is only about right now for us, and it's what I want too.' She couldn't deny herself this chance to be in his arms, to make love with him utterly.

Opening up about her hurts to him had taken away her last reserve. She would have this, hold this, carry this away with her, and maybe there would be pain later, but Lily refused to think about that now.

'The only thing I need to know is that this isn't an act of pity because of what I said back there in your office...' She couldn't bear to think that even an ounce of that emotion drove Zach's desire for her. 'I won't be your goodwill project, Zach. Anything but that.'

His face tightened with possessive determination. 'What you said to me mattered, because you trusted me enough to say it. I respect you more now than I ever have, because I understand how what you've been through has hurt you. I want you. I want to take away some of that hurt if I can. It has nothing to do with pity. Now, come here and let me love you.'

The room with its bank of built-in closets, the windows with gold and green drapes drawn closed, and the bed so very close to them, all faded from her mind as he drew her into his arms and began to whisper kisses onto her lips.

She wrapped her arms around his neck as she had done in the elevator, but softly, softly, and sighed as he kissed the nape of her neck. Pressed a caress of her own against the hot skin near his ear. Drew his head down to hers, and offered so much more of herself than she had believed she would ever give. To Zach. To any man.

But, oh, how could she think of *any* man? There was only Zach, and what he made her feel, and what she wanted him to feel for her. How could she hold back? Richard had never made her feel this way.

Her hands caressed the strong arms that held her close, rose to his shoulders and flexed against the muscles there.

She had imagined him raised above her, his shoulders bared to her touch. Had held him almost naked in her arms, just once, before he'd let her go. Now she would know all of it, and it was almost—*almost*—too much.

He threw back the quilt. Drew her shoes from her feet and settled her on soft ivory sheets. Kicked off his shoes and joined her. 'I want to hold you. Let me just hold you…close to my heart.'

At those wrenching words her heart melted, and any hope of guarding her feelings disappeared. This was enough. It had to be enough.

'Let *me* hold *you*.' She touched his face, the starkness and heat and the rasp of his skin. Drew in her breath, taking the scent of him deep inside, to a place in her memory that would never forget. She didn't want to forget any of this. Not a moment of it. In her heart, she knew she wouldn't.

Was this love? Real love? The for ever, all-encompassing kind? This deep, abiding need for him that had grown and shaped itself into something that lived with her, breathed with her, as much a part of her as her own deepest thoughts or secrets?

She had never cared for Richard like this, even when she'd tried to blind herself to his true personality. Now he was a formless shadow, less than a tendril of mist in the recesses of her mind. Zach owned it all.

Zach drew her in so close that their bodies touched, melded to each other perfectly, and then he lifted up above her, and looked down into her face through hazel eyes that shone with sweet, tender desire. And he kissed her slowly, druggingly, and she melted. Melted completely away…

'Lily of the valley. Beautiful, delicate and sweet. Will you fortify my soul?' The words poured out of Zach from a deep, still place that ached for only her. That needed her in ways he was only beginning to know.

He looked deep into her eyes, and began the slow and sensual task of removing every barrier that separated them. Shaking fingers opened the buttons on her blouse. Caressed soft, butter-yellow lace and warm creamy skin beneath.

He swallowed hard, biting back words that welled up. Promises and hopes and dreams, and things that he had denied himself years ago. That he had given up willingly because honour demanded it, but now there was this. 'I don't deserve this. I don't deserve *you*.'

Torn, longing, hungry, he cupped her face in his hands, stroked the soft skin. Watched her eyes darken as she leaned into that touch. Lowered his mouth to kiss her again because he couldn't do anything else.

Long moments later, he drew back enough to say, 'You take my breath away. Tell me again that you want this. Tell me you want it as much as I do.'

'I want to make love with you more than you'll ever be able to imagine or dream.' With those simple words, she felled him.

Emotion welled, wrapped around his heart, and even though his body ached for her something deep inside ached and longed so much more.

Her hands rose in tentative exploration. Colour stained her cheeks as she met his gaze. 'Since that night at the Manor House Inn, since long before it, I've dreamed of this. Of being able to touch your skin, to see you above me…'

'Then touch me. Look at the body that wants you so much.' He helped her with the buttons of his shirt. Then he shrugged it off. Let it drop to the floor.

Her hands ran lightly over him. Touching, caressing, knowing him, until he felt he had always been hers, and she his.

When the last piece of clothing fell away, he looked at her and words crowded up and poured out. 'Let me show you how beautiful you are.'

And he gave her all the need and hunger that had built inside him as each day had etched her deeper into his senses, his thoughts, his emotions. He may not have the words. May not be able to promise her for ever, but he would give her this, and his fulfilment would be in hers.

Lily opened her mind, her spirit and her body to Zach in the only way she could. Utterly. Totally. And when he had loved her absolutely, gaze locked to her gaze, hands and body reverencing her until they lay twined in each other's arms in shattered stillness at last, she finally admitted the truth.

She loved him. Right down to the depths of her heart and spirit and soul, in a way she had never loved before, and never would again. The realisation brought a gasping sob to her throat. She choked it back, but a small sound escaped.

'What is it?' Zach whispered the question, and brushed his mouth across hers. Touched her hair with gentle fingers, and clasped his hand over hers where it rested on his chest.

Could he know what she had discovered? Had she revealed the truth as they made love? Had it shone from her eyes? Could he possibly share those feelings?

His heart beat steadily beneath her fingertips, and he tucked her closer still in an intimacy that gave comfort, even as she struggled to come to terms with her new-found knowledge.

Lily pushed the thoughts away. She wouldn't think about her discovery or ask questions. Not yet. Right now, she was too vulnerable. She would want to believe too easily that this had changed everything, when they both had agreed that it wouldn't.

'It's nothing.' Shadows danced against the curtained windows, and danced at the edges of her heart and mind. She closed her eyes to the shadows at his windows, and distanced herself from those lying in wait at the edges of her heart. 'It's nothing at all.'

Instead, she embraced the comfort of his closeness. Nestled to his side. As he stroked his fingers across her shoulders, against her neck, through her hair, a soft lassitude stole though her.

When Lily woke, the shadows had lengthened. There must have been a tree outside the window, for long, gnarled arms seemed to reach right into the room ready to snatch her into their dry, crackling hold.

Disturbed by the mental image, she eased away from Zach's slumbering form, and paused to look down into the face now relaxed in sleep. A band tightened around her heart. How she wanted to wake beside him every day! To reach for him, and be drawn into his arms and welcomed. Making love had changed everything for her, but Zach had made his attitude clear before they did this.

Why can't you love me and want me for ever, Zach? Why can't I be enough for you to overcome those choices you've made about your life?

Heart sore, she gathered her belongings and drew away to the other end of the house. She used her cell phone to order a taxi, then tidied herself in the guest bathroom and let herself out of the house.

He hadn't made promises. This had been

their beginning, and now it was their end. No matter how much that knowledge hurt her, she had no choice but to accept it.

'Come on, Lily, answer for me. You're my last hope.' *I need you with me while I face this.*

The inner admission of that need came freely to Zach, but it was a revelation that couldn't be examined now. He stood in the middle of his mother's living room and gripped the cordless phone in tight fingers. His brother had been gone since eight this morning. Over nine long hours, and nobody had seen him.

His mother wrung her hands. 'I should have seen him onto the bus. No, I should have driven him to and from school every day myself.'

Zach shook his head. 'There's never been a hint of trouble. I've only just got around to vetting the people who walk onto my floor at work. Why us?' Theirs was a wealthy family, but certainly not the wealthiest, or the only one around.

'Hello?' Lily's voice, slightly hoarse, came at last.

She had left him after their lovemaking, after

the most wonderful and moving moments he had experienced in his life, and had slipped away while he slept. Before he'd had time to come to terms with the hurt of that, or wonder at her reasoning or his own feelings, his mother had phoned in distress because Daniel was missing.

'It's Zach. Daniel's been gone since early this morning. We can't—we haven't been able to track him down.'

'Oh, Zach. I'm coming. I'll get a taxi straight away.'

The band around his chest eased the tiniest bit. 'I'm at Mum's house.'

'Give me the address. I'm not sure if it's in my diary. I'll leave right now.' After he rattled off the address, she drew a hurried breath. 'Daniel will come back to you safe and sound, Zach. He has to, because you love him so much.'

Those words echoed through Zach's thoughts as he paced the floor. Between them, he and his mother had contacted every conceivable person who might have known where Daniel had gone, what had happened to him. And they had discovered he hadn't been seen since before school.

'What more can we do?' His mother seemed

to read his mind. She sprang up from the sofa to pace the floor, then moved to the window to stare out. 'I can't even tell if any of his casual clothes are missing, so I don't know whether he *planned* to go somewhere other than school today, or something…worse happened.'

Her mouth tightened. 'I should know every stitch of clothing he owns. A younger mother would be able to remember.'

'Don't do that to yourself.' He gave her a brief hug. 'I couldn't tell you everything that's in my own wardrobe, let alone anyone else's.'

'Oh, Zach.' She leaned into him briefly before drawing away.

'If it's a kidnapping, and they plan to contact us with ransom conditions, we could put him in jeopardy by contacting the police.' He stared out the window onto the street. 'If we *don't* contact the police, our resources are limited and we may be wasting precious time that could be spent by the authorities in trying to locate him.'

'I'm going to look through his room again.' His mother was still there when Lily arrived.

Zach watched Lily alight from the taxi and pay the driver, then hurry towards the front of the house. He opened the door before she could ring the bell. She looked straight into his eyes. A moment later, her arms were around his waist, and he was gripping her hard, close.

'I got here as quickly as I could.' She released him and stepped back, and he noticed that her eyes were red-rimmed and puffy. She looked like she had been crying long before he'd called her, and there was only one likely reason for that.

A reason he had been trying to forget since he'd first held her naked in his arms. They couldn't go on, because nothing had changed for him, even though he wished that were different.

Not now, you can't think of it now.

Her gaze searched his face. 'Is there any news?'

'Nothing. Come in. Mum will be glad to see you.'

Lily followed Zach inside his mother's house. Would Anne Swift be happy to see her? Or would she resent the intrusion, and feel that as an outsider to her family Lily shouldn't be here?

One look at Anne's tight, distressed face as she emerged from a room set off the hallway, and Lily forgot everything but the need to comfort her and help her.

Anne reached out a tremulous hand.

Lily squeezed it, and led Anne to sit on the living-room sofa.

After she took her seat beside Anne, she turned her gaze to Zach once more. 'What do you know for certain about Daniel's disappearance so far?'

Zach stood at the window and outlined all they had done. He explained that an aunt and uncle were at his house even now, in case Daniel happened to turn up there. Or someone else tried to contact Zach there about the boy.

'Have you contacted the police?' Lily hardly dared to say it aloud.

'Not yet.' Zach's shoulders tensed. 'We'll have to do it soon, if nothing else happens.'

Lily wanted to hold Zach and never let go. She wanted to pour encouragement and hope into him, and tell him not to give up. 'How much longer will you wait?'

'We'll wait until six p.m. If there's nothing by then—'

'That gives us almost half an hour.' She drew her notebook and a pencil from her bag and beckoned Zach over. 'Draw the curtains wide. We'll all be able to see anyone approaching. We need to go over every conversation, every social outing, all Daniel's school projects, and friends' parties, anything that might give us a clue.'

For the next twenty minutes, Zach and his mother turned their minds inside out as they considered all that had been happening in Daniel's life. The picture that emerged to Lily was of a boy who had changed from gregarious and outgoing, to more serious and quiet. Yet he hadn't struck her as unhappy. 'What were you like as a ten and eleven-year-old, Zach? What did you want out of life then?'

'I played with school friends, loved to kick a footy around, didn't care too much about my studies.' He gave his mother a wry glance. 'Homework time was a bit of a trial, but I eventually pulled myself together and got serious.'

'Did you get serious at Daniel's current age? When you were facing the looming thought of high school?' Something whispered at the edges of Lily's mind, nagging at her. If she could just pin it down…

Zach's eyebrows rose. He looked at Lily, then at his mother. 'Yeah. I changed a lot around that age. I got really interested in maths and commerce, actually.'

Lily's heart began to thump, but what if she was wrong? It was the wildest thought, with so little to back it up. Nevertheless, she said it. 'What if Daniel's attitude has been changing, and you haven't noticed? What if he's gone from being a young sports nut, playing with his friends, to a serious boy considering his future?'

Anne leaped to her feet. 'Oh, he has become serious. He has changed a lot in the past few months, but how does this help us?'

'He wanted to go to a Melbourne boarding school to study mechatronics.' The words finally burst from Lily. Somehow, they were all on their feet, and she turned to Zach hopefully. 'You vetoed the idea, but do you think he accepted that? Did you find some local classes for him to attend? How did he respond to the offer of those?'

Zach's face tightened. 'I made a couple of enquiries, but came up blank. I told him there were no classes available and forgot about it. I thought it was just a whim of his.'

Anne gasped, and her eyes widened. 'Daniel didn't say anything to me. Why would he want to go so far away from here? From his family?'

A silence stretched as mother and son looked at each other. Shared the concern and pain, and a dose of self-recrimination.

Lily broke that silence, but not before accepting that the bond of commitment and love they shared was nothing she had known, or would ever know. 'Is it possible that Daniel might have tried to make his way to that Melbourne boarding school on his own? Might his desire to attend there next year have driven him to do that, if he believed the chance had been refused him?'

'We have to consider it.' Zach snapped it out.

His mother spoke at the same time. 'What if he's not still there, or didn't even go?'

'I'll find out. I'll hire a private plane. That'll be the fastest.' Zach lifted the phone, and then turned to his mother. 'Use your cell phone to alert the train and bus services and the airports again. Especially anything coming back from Melbourne. Their security people are to watch for him in case he's already on his way back.

'We have to follow this possibility. It makes more sense than anything else so far, and you'll be here in case the phone rings…or anything.'

A movement outside drew Lily's gaze. She stared, then gasped at the sight of a boy with a gangling build dressed in a tee-shirt and jacket and a pair of grey school trousers, moving up the pathway with his shoulders hunched, his backpack almost dragging on the ground as he lugged it along beside him. A taxi drove away behind him. 'Daniel…'

Anne's head snapped up. Her gaze flew to the window. Then, with an inarticulate cry, she ran for the door.

Zach made a wrenching sound that etched itself across Lily's heart, and hurried behind his mother.

'Daniel! Where have you been? Are you safe, son?' Anne snatched the boy into her arms, and pulled him into the haven of their home. She drew back to look deep into his eyes.

Then it was Zach's turn to pull the boy close, and if Daniel had believed he would soon be able to break free of his brother's hold, to over-power him in a struggle of strength, the grip of Zach's arms around him now would put that belief to rest for a very long time.

Lily watched them from just paces away, but in her heart the distance was deserts wide, oceans deep. Even if Zach decided he wanted more than his career and this family, Lily could never compete. She knew nothing of this kind of love.

Finally, Zach let go of Daniel, swallowed hard several times and seemed about to speak.

Daniel spoke first, addressing himself to his mother, although one hand held a fistful of the back of Zach's shirt, something Lily felt certain the boy didn't realise he was doing.

'I'm sorry, Mum. I wanted to go away to Sarrenden College, and when Zach said no I decided to go and see it for myself so I could convince him to let me.' Daniel swallowed hard.

His voice trembled as he went on. 'Then I realised I was wrong to try to do it that way, and I tried to come home. I wanted to be back before you started worrying, but I got mixed up with the trains and I lost my cell phone, and I was scared I'd run out of money if I wasn't careful.'

'Oh, Daniel.' Anne lost her fight at last, and tears tracked down her round cheeks.

Daniel broke away from his brother and put his arms around her. A sob escaped. 'Sorry, Mum. *I'm sorry.*'

Zach stepped forward, and patted both brother and mother with large, strong hands that Lily now saw had learned their gentleness here in the heart of the loving family that had shaped him.

When Daniel drew back, and Zach laid a hand on his brother's shoulder and squeezed, Lily's heart squeezed with it.

'I'm the one who needs to apologise, Dan.' A muscle spasmed in Zach's jaw. 'For not listening to you, for brushing off your attempts to talk properly about it all. The truth is, I didn't want you to leave, but I have to learn to let you go. I'm just glad you're safe now, because you're very precious to us.'

Anne wiped her eyes, took a deep breath, and added her words of assurance, and sterner ones for the way Daniel had put himself at risk. 'This family will be making some changes in terms of keeping *all* of us safe in future. We've been so busy just living a simple family life that we've forgotten we're also worth a lot of money, and could therefore end up prey to blackmailers or worse.'

Zach nodded.

Daniel stood with head bowed inside their small circle of love. Then he looked up with a new maturity in his eyes. 'You're right, Mum. I hadn't thought about that. I wouldn't want anything to happen to you or to Zach.'

At that moment, Lily finally broke free of the stillness that had held her in place since

Daniel's return, and accepted the utter truth that this was no place for her. She couldn't even maintain a reasonable relationship with her parents, and never had been able to.

While the family were busy with each other, she slipped outside to take her second taxi ride away from the man who owned her heart.

CHAPTER THIRTEEN

LILY walked into work the next morning dressed in a severe black skirt and skin-tight green top, and wearing a set of carved wooden bangles on her right arm.

Zach watched her enter the outer office, her chin high, her shoulders stiff and her face closed against any show of emotion. 'Good morning, Lily.'

'Hello.' She rounded her desk to put her bag away. Her face softened slightly when she turned to look at him and asked after Daniel's health. 'How is your brother? Does he seem all right after his gruelling day yesterday?'

'He's okay. Mum's keeping him at home, and they're going to spend the day looking into his options for boarding school next year.' He hesitated before he took a step towards her. 'Lily, about what we shared—'

'There's no need to talk about it.' She reached for the first file he had placed on the desk. 'We had a wonderful experience together, but we both know there's no future in it. I'm here to work, now, until my contract is over. Let's focus on that.'

Zach didn't want to agree, but he sensed if he tried to argue right now she would ignore everything he said. And he didn't know fully what he *wanted* to say. Only that making love with her had left more things unresolved between them than ever before, and that he didn't want their closeness to end there.

He gave a tight nod, and walked into his own room.

'What are you both doing here?' Lily looked up from her computer screen and stared at her parents in blank question.

If it wasn't the welcome they had anticipated, she couldn't help that.

Zach must have heard her greet her parents, because he emerged from his office and came to stand at the side of her desk. The show of solidarity, even in the face of the tense relations between them, made her acknowledge the impossibility of pushing him out of her heart.

How could she do that, when he was more firmly entrenched there now than ever?

'We were in Sydney, and thought we'd drop by.' Her mother made this unlikely pronouncement.

Lily unconsciously toyed with the bangles on her arm. Her mother's gaze followed the movement, and her jaw dropped before she looked away again with an expression of distaste. So, okay, the bangles were a bit garish. But Lily realised something just then.

Her mother would look away in the face of anything about her daughter that caused her discomfort. Lily knew and understood that about Dorothea now, in a way she never had before. The knowledge was almost releasing.

Until her mother turned to Zach and pasted an entirely different expression on her face. 'Actually, our stopping by the office today has a two-fold reason. Naturally, we wanted to check on Lily and ensure she wasn't causing you any… That she was comfortable here, and settled into her work.'

Lily's father cleared his throat and looked unhappy. He took a step closer to the desk, then stopped as if uncertain how to proceed. 'I'm sure you're showing the highest standards as always, my dear. You've always done so.'

Lily's heart cracked open a little.

'Well, enough of Lily's progress.' Her mother slapped it shut again.

Why had Lily never seen that there was nothing beneath her mother's surface except more of what was on top? Lily had gravitated to her father's side, had aligned herself to him by attending his university, by trying to please him with her grades. He hadn't been as harsh, although he was by no means openly affectionate.

'You said there were two reasons you stopped by, Mum. What was the other thing?'

Dorothea stepped forward, and Lily noticed the elaborate hairstyle that must have taken hours with a hairdresser.

Her mother addressed her words to Zach. 'Carl and I are invited to a most prestigious function.' Here she paused, as though to strengthen the impact of her next words. 'We're to dine with the State Governor, and as the invitations are for ourselves and a guest each we came here to invite you, Zach, to attend with us.'

As though realising her faux pas, she turned quickly to her daughter. 'You too, Lily.'

'Unfortunately, Lily and I will have to decline your invitation.' Zach ground the words through teeth that threatened to crack under the pressure of his clamped jaw.

Something did, indeed, crack inside him as he stared at the woman who had produced such a stunning, kind, giving, amazing daughter.

'But I'd like to extend an invitation to both of you. To a special event of my own that happens to be on in…' he heard himself say '…a little under an hour from now. My family will be there, and I'd like you and Carl to meet them. What do you say?'

When Dorothea looked trapped and uncertain, he said, quite mildly he thought, 'Don't concern yourself about time frames. This will only take about an hour. You'll be gone and back to your hotel with plenty of time to prepare for your night out.'

'Well, that's very kind of you, but are you certain you can't see your way to attending the dinner with us?' Dorothea didn't quite manage to hide her disappointment.

'Quite certain,' he said, and wondered if he was completely insane. 'But that doesn't mean I have to forego the pleasure of your company altogether.'

A choked sound from Lily drew his gaze to her.

'Will you come with me?' He watched her toy with some papers on her desk, and willed her to look at him. 'You don't have to.'

Finally, she looked up and their gazes met.

She glanced once at her mother, then brought her gaze back to his face and nodded agreement. 'I'll come.' Her half-shrug was meant to indicate she didn't care one way or the other, but tension bracketed the sides of her mouth. 'It's still work time for another hour, anyway.'

'Get your bag, then. We'll lock up here, escort your parents downstairs and see them into a taxi, then meet them at my venue.' Where Lily and her parents would spend an hour with his mother and brother. Was that why he was doing it?

Probably. It was past time her parents saw a real family in action. It might give them a clue about how it should be done! And her father had seemed…different. As though he had really wanted to see her. Well, it was too late to take the invitation back.

Zach was out of control right now, acting rashly, and he knew it. Something was building up inside him. He didn't know what it was, but a physical outlet for all that growing tension couldn't hurt. He would take what relief he could get.

Outside the building, Lily shivered as he hailed a taxi, opened the door, and waited while her parents climbed inside. Zach gave the driver the directions and a generous fare, and sent the cab on its way before either parent managed a word.

As the taxi merged into the traffic, he turned to Lily. 'Let's get to my car. I've got a warm jacket I can lend you.'

She didn't budge from the footpath. 'I agreed to come, but that's because of my parents. Where are we going?'

'To my touch-footy practice at French's Park oval. You probably think I'm mad.'

'Yes, I do, actually.'

She didn't speak again. Just got into the car when they reached it, and when he handed her the jacket out of his kit she wrapped it around her shoulders.

Zach's tension spiked higher. He wanted to be that comforting blanket in Lily's life. He wanted to be all sorts of things to her.

When they arrived at the park, he pulled his

kit bag out of the back seat and slung it over his shoulder.

Then he turned to look at Lily, and it just happened. One minute he was watching the wind play with her hair, and wanting that hair spread across his pillow as it had been so recently. The next, love for her slammed through him, almost knocking him to his knees.

He had been so stupid, so blind, and now that blindfold was off and he knew. Knew that he loved her, knew that every second in her arms when they made love had been about showing her, convincing her, giving all of that love to her, even though he hadn't realised it then himself.

He wanted to say things to her, life-altering things. *Have my baby. Be my lover for ever.* Zach wanted to say other things, too. Things like *marry me*.

How? How could he say those things? His ex-fiancée hadn't hesitated to tell him it was his commitment to his family that had ruined things for them, and Zach cared about Lily so much more than he had ever cared for Lara. Yet Lily was so different to Lara. And she loved his family.

'There are my parents, and your mother and Daniel.' Lily gestured towards a rustic shelter. Tin roof, upright support timbers. It had little else to recommend it.

Zach reluctantly followed Lily's gaze. 'They don't usually attend my practice sessions, but after yesterday I guess we all wanted to be close.'

Now he had thrown Lily's family into the middle of that closeness. Zach's thoughts churned.

When a team mate yelled for him to get togged up and get on the field, Zach turned to Lily and said harshly, because of the confusion reigning inside, 'I have to go. Mum will look after you.'

He wanted to stay at Lily's side and sort out his feelings right now. But again that team mate called, and he reluctantly ran onto the field.

Zach practised football like a madman. This was Lily's observation as she tore her gaze from the strong legs displayed to advantage in a pair of dark blue shorts as he ran all over the field. He treated the football like an enemy he wanted to dispatch.

And she loved him. Loved everything about him. Even his obsession with a game that appeared to involve nothing more than butting shoulders with his colleagues, and seeing if he could knock any of them to the ground, then trying to avoid being knocked flat himself.

She watched him run to the other end of the field in pursuit of someone she had thought was actually on his own side. 'I thought touch football was supposed to be non-aggressive.'

'It's appalling, is what it is, and, oh, look. Now it's started to rain!' Her mother's sharp words were the first she had uttered since before the game began.

After meeting Zach's family, she had stood in speechless silence, too taken aback apparently by the outcome of Zach's invitation to be able to say anything coherent.

'Uh-oh.' Daniel's grin still held some shadows. He stood close to his mother, and had one arm draped loosely around her shoulders. He nevertheless cast a reluctantly admiring glance in his brother's direction. 'Looks like we're in for some mud and swearing.'

The eyebrows Lily's mother plucked so finely hiked into her coiffed and lacquered hair. 'I beg your pardon?'

Daniel just grinned and turned his attention back to the field, where Zach and his colleagues did indeed appear to have transformed into mud-worshipping, loud-mouthed heathens.

Lily bit back a gasp as Zach performed a rather spectacular slide on his tummy right through a big, muddy puddle to stop the ball getting over the end line. 'He's acting like a maniac. He'll hurt himself. He could break his ribs doing that.'

'Something certainly seems to have got into him today.' Anne gave Lily a searching glance.

'Ah, hmm.' Lily's father bent his head towards her, his face tight, eyes uncertain, and said so no one would hear, 'I looked into your agency business, visited your website. And I read your staff recruitment policy.'

'Did you?' She hadn't meant to sound shocked, but she was. 'Why?'

'So when I complimented you on your business acumen and success, you'd believe it when I said that I'm proud of you.' For a moment, his eyes shone with what might have been the hint of some deep emotion. 'I miss you at the university. It's not the same without you. We could be ourselves there without… As for that Pearce, well, your mother liked him but I don't. Never have, really, but I thought you cared for him.'

His voice dropped to a near whisper. 'I'm a weak man, Lily. I can't walk away, and I'm no match for—'

'It's all right.' Her hand closed on his wrist.

He gave a tense cough. 'I could visit, if you'd like. I've got several trips to Sydney planned in the course of this university year.'

'That would be nice.' She swallowed hard on the emotion that had risen, squeezed his hand and let it go. Followed his regretful glance to her mother, and gave a slight shake of her head. 'We are what we are, Dad. Let's just try to look forward, not back any more.'

Her father nodded and looked away, back out to the field where the game had wound down and the rain had stopped, leaving a puddle in the middle of the field, and a bunch of very grubby businessmen to hobble off that field in various states of exhaustion and bruises.

After a moment of silence, her dad turned back to her. 'Do you love him, Lilybell?'

She reached up and dropped a shaky kiss

on his whiskery cheek. 'It can't work out between us, Dad, but yes. I love him. I can't seem to help it.'

From a distance, Zach observed the exchange between Lily and her father. The bent heads, the way she reached up to kiss the older man's cheek.

Her mother looked disgruntled, but this fact didn't seem to be bothering anyone but Dorothea herself.

Mud dripped from Zach's elbow as he approached and nodded to Lily's parents. 'I hope you've enjoyed the time with Lily, and thank you for taking the opportunity to meet my family. I'd introduce you to my team mates, who happen to be business colleagues, except it appears they're all anxious to get home and rid themselves of their muddy clothes.'

The park had a changing room, but not showers.

Zach gave his mother an air hug.

She grasped his arm before he could move away, and asked, 'What are you doing, Zachary?'

'I'm starting to realise some things I should have understood long ago, Mum.' Purpose filled him as he turned to Lily. 'Are you ready to leave?'

She dipped her head in agreement, said quick farewells to her parents, then to his mother and Daniel.

Did Lily love him, as Zach loved her? His heart burned to know the answer at the same time he feared it. If she didn't…

After Zach changed clothes, they made their way to her home in silence. When they arrived, Lily got out of the car quickly and hurried to her door.

Zach followed. 'Don't say goodbye yet.' He clenched his fists as he fought the need to reach for her. They had to talk first. He had to tell her what he had realised out there on the football field, and hope she returned his feelings.

'Why not? The day is over. What's there to say that hasn't already been said?' She turned fully to face him. Her eyes held the shadows of all that had passed between them. Lily opened the apartment door.

Before she could try to stop him, Zach drew her inside and stepped in too. On the sofa in the small living room, Jemima the cat raised a furry head, gave an interested rumble, and subsided again.

Zach attempted a wry smile. 'We forgot to watch for her, despite your sign on the door.'

'Forgetting is what I do best.' Her words were flippant, but he heard the bitter edge, and wanted to tell her not to be so hard on herself.

In some part of his mind, Zach noticed the warmth and cosiness of Lily's home, and his heart ached to be part of that warmth. That comfort. Was it possible? Would she even consider it?

'Lily.' He held her gaze, despite the wariness in her eyes. 'I was wrong to believe what Lara said to me five years ago. I realise now that I didn't even love her.' Love? He hadn't even known the meaning of the word until Lily had stormed his life and heart with her notebook and her pencil at the ready in her hands.

Lily took a slow breath. 'What exactly did Lara say that you shouldn't have believed?'

'That I couldn't have my family and have her, too. That I gave them all my time and attention and there wasn't enough left for her.' There were sticky notes on Lily's refrigerator in date order, left to right, row after row, outlining things she had to remember and do. A wall chart covered the area over the sink.

Two Bendigo pottery mugs sat side by side

on the counter. Zach wanted to drink coffee with her out of matching mugs in the mornings for the rest of their lives.

His hands clenched at his sides. 'I believed what Lara told me. I thought I didn't have enough to offer any woman, that loving someone and caring for my family were mutually exclusive because I couldn't abandon them to focus on the woman in my life. But Lara was wrong.'

Lily's lips parted on a soundless breath. 'After seeing you all together the day Daniel went missing, I understand how close you are. I'm certain Lara was *right*. How could anyone else fit into what you all share?'

'You already fit in. You helped organise my birthday party, watched Dan play hockey, and stood in the rain to watch me play at practice today. You were there when Dan went missing. You've already proved you can be a willing part of my family.' All along, Lily had been fitting into his life and Zach had been too stupid, too scared to realise the truth until now.

He took a deep breath and held her gaze, his body tense as he watched for her reaction. 'I love you, Lily. You have my heart and I want to marry you and keep you in my life as my wife, my lover, *and* as part of my family.'

Lily choked back a gasp. Zach spoke with such intensity. There were lines of strain on his face that hadn't been there before. She wanted to smooth those tense places with the tips of her fingers. Wanted to put her arms around him and hold onto him and never let go.

She wanted to say yes to him, but they couldn't be together, no matter what he said. 'I can't. I don't—'

'You don't love me?' His mouth tightened, and he took another step towards her. He seemed to reach right into the depths of himself, to struggle before he finally said, his voice deep and hungry and determined, 'I don't believe that. I know you, and I love you, and I believe you love me too. It was there in every touch, every moment, when I took you back to my house and we made love. Are you going to tell me I'm wrong about that?'

Lily couldn't deny it, but she had to make him see the reality. He might think he loved her now, but, when he realised how much her injury really impacted on her life, he would change his mind. He wouldn't be able to remain committed to her then.

She tugged her hands from his, flung one arm out to encompass her home, pointed at the fridge with its notes stuck all over it. 'How can you want to be with this? Take a good look, Zach, and see that it's so much more than you've thought about or realised.'

When he didn't seem to get her point, she grabbed him by the arm and dragged him across to the room beyond the tiny bathroom.

She flung that door open, and gestured at the floor-to-ceiling shelves that covered one wall. They were already half-filled with notebooks, each one labelled and dated.

'My notebooks have glossaries, Zach, and I refer to them.' She sent another wild gesture towards the shelves. 'Sometimes I have to come in here and go through that wall of books and try to figure out what I've done or said, or where I've been or where I'm supposed to be going.'

'Don't.' He choked it out. Reached for her. Pulled her into his arms and wrapped them around her, and gave a harsh, aching sob of sound into her hair. *'Don't*, Lily. *It doesn't matter.'*

She wrapped her arms around his waist. Oh, blissful homecoming. Pressed her head to his chest, and listened to a heartbeat that would be part of her own for ever.

But this still couldn't be, and she drew back

in his arms. Forced her gaze up until it reached his eyes. Love shone there. 'It matters, Zach. How can it not?'

'Yes, okay, fine, it matters, but not in the way you're saying!' He dropped his arms. Turned away from her on an abrupt movement that took him to those shelves. He looked his fill, and then he looked at her. 'Don't you see? You've got my whole heart right now, and you'll always have it. You can come *into* the circle of my family and be with me there.'

'But…'

'You're the one who's really backing away.' He said it on a breath of revelation, and stared at her with dawning understanding. 'I've been so wrapped up in fighting my own fears that it didn't occur to me you'd set up your own road-blocks, but you have.'

'They're not just roadblocks, Zach.' She thought back over the struggles she had endured. The battles she had fought to get her life back after her accident. Some she had won. Others had defeated her and always would. 'They're impenetrable walls.'

He glared at her, and those hands were fisted again and he made no effort to hide his anger or his accusation. 'You're hiding behind your memory condition to avoid committing to me, to us.' He drew a hard breath. 'You've always done that. It's why you refuse to work anywhere for longer than a few weeks.

'It's not simply because you're scared they'll notice you're different and that might make things uncomfortable. You're not worried about making mistakes and getting things wrong. It's because you believe, when they realise your condition, they'll reject *you*.'

'All right. I admit it!' Goaded, she flung her words at him like arrows, only it was Cupid in reverse, because this could only end it. 'I admit, I won't stay at anything too long. I'm scared if I do the people around me will realise I'm not like others, and won't want me any longer. I'm scared about that because it's *true*. I'm *different*. Less. *Not good enough!*'

For a moment, Lily struggled to control her emotions. She would not cry in front of him. 'If I opened myself to you right now, if I agreed to stay and love you for ever, you'd give up on me. Just like Mum did. Just like Richard did.'

'Listen to me.' He pulled her to his chest. 'Listen.'

She struggled, but he refused to let her go, and she subsided against him with a cry that mingled pain and the pieces of a life she had put together by her own might and determination, but that was still, oh, so fragile.

'I'm not them.' Zach breathed the words against Lily's ear. Beneath her hand, they reverberated in his chest, too. His words were all around her, and she couldn't reject them. He seemed determined that she wouldn't.

Then he drew her closer still. With a shaking hand, he cupped the back of her neck, stroked his fingers through her hair. He closed his eyes, pressed his cheek to hers and swallowed hard. 'I love you. I need you. *You*, Lily, just as you are. You're not less. You're *more*. So much more.'

Zach drew back, his gaze searching hers. 'I told you I want to marry you. I mean that. Your memory loss only makes me love you more. It's part of you, Lily, part of all that I love about you.'

Oh, how her heart soared before she dragged it back down and forced herself to tell the truth, to make him see all of it. 'It will never change, Zach. Every day for the rest of my life, I'll get out of bed and find my notebook sitting there with a sticky note on top telling me to record everything that matters.'

Her breath caught, but she forced herself to go on. 'I'll wash my hair and then not be able to remember if I did it or not. Clothes will go missing because I take them to the dry-cleaners and don't remember they're there. Little things will keep falling through the cracks in my brain.'

'We'll get shower-proof sticky notes and a waterproof pen. You can write down when you wash your hair.' His gaze roved over her. Softly. Oh, so softly. 'I'll remind you about the dry-cleaners. Hell, Lily, I wouldn't care if we lost every stitch of clothing we owned. It doesn't matter if you forget things. I'll remind you of what I can, and for the rest we'll just get over it. *I want you. That's all that matters.*'

Finally, hope took hold. Found fertile soil and put down its roots. Blossomed as her hands lifted, reaching for the man who had taken her heart, and would have it always. 'I…I love you. If you're sure about this—'

'*Lily.*' He clasped her hands. Rained kisses over her face. His eyes filled with tears and he laughed, blinked them back, fell on her mouth and kissed her with passion and longing and hunger. 'My Lily of the valley, my tiger Lily and Lily of peace. I'm not letting you go. Not ever. Do you understand that?'

He touched beneath her lashes where tears had pooled and spilled over. Kissed those tears away. Looked into her eyes and gave her his promise. 'I'm going to learn all about your memory condition, but not because I pity you. I'll do it because I want your life to be happy and secure and comfortable, and I'm determined to help you make it that way.'

'What about your family? Will they really be able to accept me?' As his wife?

Zach dropped a kiss on her brow, and a smile broke out on his face. 'They already think you're great. I know they'll welcome you into all our lives.'

'Together.' Could she really be a part of a loving family? Have that, and the man at her side? 'Oh, Zach. Is this really happening? Is it really all true?'

He took her latest notebook from its resting place on her desk. Flipped it open, and scribbled for a long time inside it before he snapped it shut. 'It's true, and in case you ever forget I've just written down for you that you agree to be part of my family.

'Sunday dinners at Mum's place. Visits to

Dan at his school next year. Entertaining him when he's home. We'll do it together, Lily. Say you'll marry me soon.'

'I love you so much. I want to marry you.' Her heart pounded hard in her chest as hope and happiness welled up. But there was one last thing. 'What about…children of our own? I don't know if I can be a good mother.'

He laughed. Wrapped his arms around her and hugged her up tight against him, and then his laughter faded and he looked deep into her eyes and let his love shine. 'I want babies with you. We'll muddle through. Together.'

They were the sweetest words Lily had ever heard. 'Then yes, Zach, I want to marry you.'

'Soon.' He growled the command and scooped her up and into his arms, then crossed to her bedroom and flung open the door. 'Marry me soon, but make love to me right now.'

And that is exactly what she did.

EPILOGUE

'I'D like to say a few words before we head for the beach, and the fun part of the day for the younger contingent.' Zach stood at the long, elegant restaurant table and felt Lily's hand slip into his where she sat beside him.

It was the beginning of summer. After a Las Vegas wedding—he'd refused to wait and Lily, bless her, had agreed—they'd now been married eight wonderful months. Every day he wondered how he had got to be so blessed.

Today, his heart was bursting. And breaking a little, too. The expression in Lily's eyes showed she understood it all. She squeezed his hand.

Today was primarily about Daniel, and they had worked hard to ensure it would be memorable for him. Daniel's small group of young mates fell silent now, and looked at Zach expectantly.

Zach glanced at the rest of the guests. At Lily's parents who, at her father's instigation, were seeing her more often, even if relations would probably never be picture-perfect. Her mother was learning to curb her tongue, particularly when her husband told her in a quavering voice to do exactly that!

Zach's mother was accompanied by Vince Goodman today. Zach wasn't sure what he thought of that man's recurring appearance in his mother's life.

Lily's work colleagues, five lovely women aged between twenty-something to Deborah's 'young' forty, ranged beside her at the table. And there was Maddie, back from her time off months ago, and running Zach's office once again. They were all here.

He cleared his throat. 'Daniel, we couldn't be more proud that you've been accepted into Sarrenden College, and we hope that the experience is everything you could want.' A smile tugged at his mouth as he looked at his young brother. 'We'd all like to get in early and request computerised robots for next Christmas, but we'd settle for your company in the school holidays.'

Laughter echoed around the table.

'Thanks, Zach. Thanks, Mum.' Daniel's grin was wide and happy, and full of his hopes and dreams. 'I can't wait to get there.' He glanced at his mates. 'But I'll be back often. Maybe we could form a recreational hockey team and meet up every holidays.'

This suggestion met with enthusiastic cheers that took a while to die down. The boys had been good, but they were starting to get twitchy now that the food was finished and they'd had their share of caffeinated fizzy drinks.

'We're going to head to Whale Beach now so we can enjoy some sun and surf.' Zach said it cheerfully, but suddenly his throat tightened. He hadn't realised it would be so hard to say this goodbye, even though Daniel wouldn't be going for quite a few weeks yet, and it wasn't as if he was moving to the other side of the world.

Zach smiled down at Lily, and wondered when his hand had tightened on hers so fiercely, and how she had known he would need that.

And he let the joy in his heart flow around the bittersweet acceptance that his little brother was growing up and needed to spread his wings. 'Before we leave the restaurant, there's another announcement.'

Zach drew Lily to her feet. He smiled with pride and pleasure at this woman who had unlocked a part of his heart he had thought closed for ever. Who had helped him to grieve for his father in ways he hadn't realised he had suppressed over all those years.

And who had let him into *her* world, and had blossomed somehow, even in the face of his bumbling attempts to be her rock, and to stand back so she could be her own strength too.

'A few months ago, Lily reapplied to finish her psychology studies. She's had a bit of shift in focus since then, but I'm very proud to say she received her acceptance letter recently.'

He saw the pride that crossed her father's face, and also the knowledge of what was about to come. Carl was the only one who knew, besides Zach and Lily herself. Sharing that particular secret had bonded them together in a special way.

Lily smiled at Zach, and then at the group of faces at the table. Her face, too, shone with pride and pleasure. 'I'm thrilled to have received that acceptance letter. It's important to me because I've proved I can do it. As you all know, Deborah has already agreed to take over most of the running of the job agency to allow me to focus on my studies.'

'My daughter was a High Distinction student,' Zach heard Dorothea brag to Maddie.

Lily heard it too, and gave a wry shake of her head. 'Well, Deb, I'm still going to need you to run the agency, and I'll still be going to classes for a while, but not at university. These will be classes of an altogether different kind.' ·

After a moment of complete silence at the table, Daniel gave an excited whoop that reverberated right through the restaurant. 'I know what she's going to say! I know it, I know it.'

'Yes.' Lily turned a smiling face towards Zach, and love and happiness shone in her eyes. 'With my business to take care of and…other things on the way, I don't feel I can go back to university studies just now. Instead, the classes I'll be attending are Lamaze.' Her voice filled with excitement and pleasure. 'Zach and I are expecting a baby!'

'Oh, my!'

'This is so wonderful!'

'I'm going to be an uncle.' This came from Daniel, of course.

Lily's mother dropped her wine glass and

splashed a hideously expensive white all over the skirt of her navy dress. She was so busy gaping, she didn't actually notice.

Lily's girls got up and did an impromptu boogie dance right there beside the table, complete with excited screams, and quite a bit of bottom wiggling.

Daniel's friends stared, open-mouthed, at the spectacle of five adult women acting crazy in a really expensive restaurant.

While Vince probably thought Zach wasn't taking notice, he kissed Zach's mother. Right on her mouth.

'Don't growl,' Lily admonished.

Zach cupped the back of her head with his hand, and let his gaze linger on eyes that shone like stars. 'I love you so much. Did I growl?'

'You were about to. I love you, too.'

'Go party.' He nodded towards the line of women still boogying behind her.

Lily joined her friends and danced around the table. Zach laughed, grabbed Maddie, who happened to be closest, and danced her around too.

His mother cried into Vince's dinner shirt.

Half a dozen almost-teenage boys thunked their heads on the table in disgust.

The other diners gawked. Some smiled, some shook their heads. But, in the end, if a little pandemonium broke out in one of Sydney's most prestigious and elite eating venues that Sunday afternoon, so what? They all seemed to have had a good time!

MILLS & BOON
Romance

On sale 1st June 2007

A MOTHER FOR THE TYCOON'S CHILD
by Patricia Thayer

Morgan finds love with gorgeous single father Justin as she battles with the legacy of her past. Don't miss the final instalment of the heartwarming ***Rocky Mountain Brides***.

THE BOSS AND HIS SECRETARY
by Jessica Steele

This is a classic office romance from a much-loved British author. When Taryn takes a job with handsome millionaire Jake she's determined not to mix business and pleasure…

BILLIONAIRE ON HER DOORSTEP
by Ally Blake

Be swept away to sunny Australia. Maggie never expected to find love in sleepy seaside Sorrento, but one day she opens her door… and knows her life will never be the same again.

MARRIED BY MORNING
by Shirley Jump

In the makeover Bride and Groom duet, playboy Carter's practical employee Daphne is certainly surprised when she finds out her boss has his eye on her…

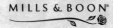

FREE

4 BOOKS AND A SURPRISE GIFT!

We would like to take this opportunity to thank you for reading this
Mills & Boon® book by offering you the chance to take FOUR more
specially selected titles from the Romance series absolutely FREE!
We're also making this offer to introduce you to the benefits of the
Mills & Boon® Reader Service™—

- ★ **FREE home delivery**
- ★ **FREE gifts and competitions**
- ★ **FREE monthly Newsletter**
- ★ **Books available before they're in the shops**
- ★ **Exclusive Reader Service offers**

Accepting these FREE books and gift places you under no obligation
to buy; you may cancel at any time, even after receiving your free
shipment. Simply complete your details below and return the entire
page to the address below. You don't even need a stamp!

YES! Please send me 4 free Romance books and a surprise gift. I
understand that unless you hear from me, I will receive 6
superb new titles every month for just £2.89 each, postage and packing
free. I am under no obligation to purchase any books and may cancel
my subscription at any time. The free books and gift will be mine to
keep in any case.

N7ZEE

Ms/Mrs/Miss/Mr..Initials ....
BLOCK CAPITALS PLEASE

Surname ....

Address ....

....

....Postcode ....

Send this whole page to:
The Reader Service, FREEPOST CN81, Croydon, CR9 3WZ